I0676258

# CHICAGO SWING

# CHICAGO
# SWING

GREGORY C. RANDALL

Printed in the United States of America

Windsor Hill Publishing, Inc.
Walnut Creek, California 94596

ISBN: 978-0-9656510-8-0

This story is dedicated to my grandmothers,
Beatrice Smith
Eva Struble

# 1

THE KID ASKED, "You sure they'll work?" as he scuffled through the newspapers and trash spread across the floor of the old stable. Looking through the cracked window above the workbench, he watched the evening lights of Chicago's skyscrapers blink and shimmer through the entangled branches of the barren trees.

"Haven't I done this a thousand times before, laddie? They will work. Didn't they make the owners squirm with fear, laddie, didn't they?"

The young fellow nodded, they had performed devilishly well. "Won't the cold make 'em not explode?"

"No, my boy, no," the older man said, his Welsh accent added a lilt to his patter. "This here cold morning's in our favor; makes the sticks more stable, less chance of going off when we hit a bump. Not like the hot summer when the little darlings sweat, then there's hell to pay, and then you're fucked."

The boy shivered under his worn canvas miner's jacket as he took a long pull on his cigarette. He watched as the older man taped the small wind-up alarm clock to the bundle of dynamite. "This, a battery and a blasting cap are all we need, boy. You drive real slow now; I'll quick step out and place this baby-girl where I need to and then as quick as a flash, I'll jump back in and away we go to our next delivery, easy as cherry pie, laddie."

The kid stood three feet away; he didn't want his cigarette to blow them both to heaven. Five devices sat on the bench, three sticks of Mr. Nobel's prize invention, a small Woolworth alarm clock and battery, a little tin foil for a switch and they were done. He watched the older man place a thin piece of tire inner tube between the bits of tin foil. "Kind of like a johnny for your dick, me'boy. Pays to be safe you know. Don't want to get pregnant, do we?" He offered the last with a smile that showed his perfect white teeth. Then he gently placed each bomb in a black shoe box, just like nesting a baby in a crib. He packed some crumpled newspapers around them. He could read *The Nation,* in bold letters above the headlines; March 1933 was legible in the upper corner. He left another stack of the socialist rag lying on the floor of the fusty garage.

"They tell me you know the town," he asked the kid.

"Been a taxi driver for the last two years; I was tossed from the mine for organizing, my uncle got me the job. Drive nights, cold fucking winter nights, looking forward to June, that'll be a nice change."

"Taxi drivers need to have a good memory, read this and memorize it. We'll start with the first drop and then proceed north. Last stop will be East Water. The whole trip isn't three miles, shouldn't take thirty minutes. These baby-girls are set to blow at 2:30, close enough for as best as these pieces of cheap shit will work. You slow down where I tell you to slow, then, as quick as a bitch-in-heat, I'll set the box and climb back in and you head to the next stop on the list. No speeding, no racing, watch the signs and lights. If you see a cop, wave. No one will stop a cab at two in the morning." He waited for the boy to read the list and then he quizzed him.

"South Wells to West Washington, then West Erie, then east to East Water Street and the last on East Grand. I'll go up

La Salle and make loops to the west side then east on Erie to St. Clair for the last two. Should be aces by 2:15."

"You did well, laddie, real good." The old man placed the five small boxes on the floor of the cab.

The boy lit another smoke from the box on the workbench, his hand shook. The haze rose to the rafters of the old garage; it had been a horse stable, it still smelled of urine.

"Did you go to church this morning, lad?"

"My mother dragged me, she says I got to pray for the miners and the other Irish comrades held under the thumb of the managers, so's I prayed. But I really prayed that we won't get caught."

"Good for you, good for you. Get your kit together, we're out of here."

They rode east on Roosevelt, across the Chicago River to Wells, then north. At the first stop, the older man placed a box near a trash bin in an alley shared by the Stratford Building and the Commonwealth Edison Company. At the second stop, he hid a box in a rear alley, under a stack of old *Tribune* newspapers, a Bell Telephone sign was posted over the service entry.

"Now cross-town," the Welshman said. They trundled noisily across the iron deck of La Salle Street Bridge and headed to Erie. At East Illinois Street, a police prowler slid to a stop next to them, the kid waved.

"Late fare?" the cop asked.

"Yes sir, and hopefully my last. If that asshole in the back has to throw up, I'll dump him on the street. I don't want to spend the night cleaning this cab; my boss will have a conniption."

The cop smiled, one Mick to another, "Drive safe."

"Yes sir, always do. Have a good night. Awfully quiet, just the way I like it."

He sped up; his passenger relaxed his hand on the revolver

in his jacket. They followed the cruiser for two blocks, then turned over one block to parallel La Salle Street as they continued north.

"Smooth, real smooth," the old man said from the backseat.

At West Erie, the kid slowed to a crawl near the Sprague Warner Grocery warehouse; the man, now with practiced ease, quickly stepped out, paralleled the cab's path and set a box to right of a steel door. He dragged a trash bin in front of the shoebox and casually slipped back into the auto.

"Only clear opening was near that fucking steel door, hope it does the trick."

They turned on Erie and headed east to St. Clair Street, then south to their last two stops, Water Street and East Grand. Both went smoothly. By 2:15, they were crossing the Michigan Avenue Bridge, heading south, back to the garage.

The watchman at the Willett Bus and Teaming Company on East Grand had already put in a long weekend. The next day was May Day. His younger brother was in a union and he remembered him saying it should be a holiday.

"Holiday my ass," the watchman had said to him. "It's just a day to fuck-off, how would you feed your family if they fired you?"

"That's why you need a union," had been his brother's curt reply.

But now he needed to get some rest and thankfully the car barn was quiet. Usually, the crews started coming in early to warm up the engines and start repairs, but that wouldn't be for three more hours. He poured the last of his coffee from his thermos. *Maybe things won't be as hectic today, until then, I think I'll get a little shut-eye.* As he crossed the last parking bay, the brick wall in front of him exploded, throwing bricks, metal furniture, and him across the room, against the side of a bus. Glass from the shattered overhead skylight fell like sharp rain, cutting his arms as he threw them over his head. Debris and dust filled the barn and as it settled a hole in the side of the building slowly materialized and where the great barn doors had been, the dim light from the street cast a grey pallor over the destruction. The watchman tried to look at his hands in the gloom; he knew they covered with blood, they felt wet and sticky. The dust made him retch; he couldn't hear anything.

Standing in the door of the old garage, the gaffer offered the boy one of his cigarettes, he took it.

"That's five salutes, good job my boy, good job; got away clean as a whistle." The man looked around, "Damn, I left my jacket in the backseat, could you grab it for me and then we can split. I left your cash on the seat, in tens."

The boy desperately needed the hundred dollars the man had promised him; they told him the bombs would go off in the early morning, no chance of anyone getting killed, just the union boss asking for a little help for a friend. "Just drive the man where he says, I don't know what he wants, but he's a good Joe," was all that was said. He had done it once before. He leaned into the car, not seeing any coat, he yelled, "No coat here."

"Got to be," the man said, sliding the revolver out of his pocket. "I sure as hell left it in there."

The kid began to stand upright, holding an envelope in his hand. The bomber calmly lifted the gun to the back of the boy's head and pulled the trigger, the boy's forehead and chunks of his brain exploded across the cab's windows, some landing on the cheap upholstery. As the boy began to fall back toward the car, the killer pushed him, face down, into the back seat; the smell of burnt hair, brains and blood blended with the smell of cigarettes. He shut the door, took the kid's envelope, folded it, and slid it into his front pocket. He wiped down every hard surface and walked to the opening of the garage. He deliberately closed the double-hinged doors, slipped a rusty padlock through the two iron rings and clicked the lock tight. He heard sirens and fire trucks echoing from downtown as he walked the two blocks to his new Ford Model B Coupe. He slid the gun under the seat and headed west, across the river.

*It was May 1st, May Day the workers called it, a day to prove their worth to management and themselves, a day to stand shoulder to shoulder with other trade unionists, anarchists, communists, and those upset with the general state of the economy and politics. Most didn't trust each other; many used every opportunity available to betray or set up another to take a fall. The Teamsters hoped that the communists would take the blame for the bombs; the communists wanted the cops to take the fall, the politicians were patient with their finger of blame. But one vengeful person wanted them all to pay.*

# 2

DETECTIVE TONY ALFANO slid a piece of cardboard under his knee to protect his suit pants as he bent close to the body. From the number of maggots in the man's nose, his body had been there at least three days. The stench was horrific. Alfano looked at the two patrolmen standing upwind.

"Which one of you mugs found him?"

"…Me, sir. …Snyder, sir."

"Don't be nervous, Snyder, just asking. What time was that?"

"…Early this morning, about 6:30. Our shift started at 6:00. We walked past and Jerry said he smelled something, he said he knew the smell from the war."

"You talk too much kid," the other patrolman said.

"I assume you are Jerry; last name, patrolman."

"…Jabrowski."

"Well, Jerry Jabrowski, tell me what you saw."

"Wasn't so much what I saw, it was what I smelled. Lots of dead bodies in the war, piles of 'em, tends to have its own odor if you know what I mean?"

"I do, I assume he wasn't all nicely displayed like this, was he?" Alfano waited three beats; he didn't have all day.

"Well, Snyder?"

"When we walked up the alley, we was coming from Washington there, the smell was real strong, wind blowing that way and all."

"Yeah, I got the smell part written down, what did you do, Jabrowski?"

"We saw this shoe sticking out from under this pile of cardboard. Still dry. Hadn't rained for four days so I figured that was how long he's been here. We cleared away the upper sheets, they's stacked over there—nothing among 'em. When we got down to his stinking body I noticed all the black blood under him, and the fact that his arm was twisted under him unnatural like."

"… Notice anything else, Snyder?"

"I noticed his coat and shirt was pulled up over his face and he had three holes in his chest."

"Well, it's not now."

"I pulled it down to look at his face, that's when I saw the maggots."

"That when you vomited?"

Snyder looked at Jabrowski, who turned away.

"Yes sir, never seen one this bad. …Kind of got me in my breakfast, sorry, sir."

"Happens even to the most callous when the situation is right. You two go and make your reports to the sergeant. Thanks, but be more careful next time."

Alfano watched the two patrolmen walk toward Madison Street, mid-morning traffic streaming by, everyone with somewhere to go. This poor sap wasn't going anywhere except to a cold slab in the morgue. He looked the opposite way, down the alley to Washington Street. He knew at least eight saloons within four blocks of this body, all currently illegal, all supplied by the mobs, all waiting for the feds to get entirely out of the liquor prohibition business. The stiff could have come from any one of them.

Alfano spent more time battling his own police department than trying to fix problems on the street. He was rigged
that way, maybe it was his mother, he didn't know. She'd been
dead twenty years, almost as long as he'd been a cop. She'd
kept him straight but poor. He knew half the department was
on the take and the other half was on the give. Sometimes he
felt like a fool, playing blind man's bluff, a game where the
rules and the players changed from month to month, sometimes it seemed like day to day. Ever since the Czech, Anton
Cermak, was elected mayor, it had gotten worse, not that the
inept Bill Thompson was all that clean. But Cermak was dead
now, killed by a crazy Italian assassin in Miami while Cermak
shook hands with Franklin Roosevelt. He had delivered Chicago's votes to Roosevelt in 1932. Roosevelt was one lucky
SOB, stray bullets hit five other people, but Mr. and Mrs. Roosevelt were unharmed. Florida's justice was swift. The killer,
Giuseppe Zangara, was fried in their electric chair just thir-
ty-three days later, setting some kind of record. Some people
said, Walter Winchell included, that Cermak was the target all
along. Rumor had it that Cermak was the target of Frank Nitti, the gangster, who was less than pleased that Cermak, using
his own personal bodyguard of Chicago cops, tried to have
him assassinated. With Cermak gone, a whole new bunch of
problems befell the city, the biggest one being: who would
take over control of the political machine built by Cermak and
his crony, Patrick Nash? Cermak had been called "the wettest
man in Chicago," by the *Tribune*. Some said he was under Al
Capone's control, but Alfano wasn't sure. But Alfano knew
one thing for sure, the dead man at his feet; he was someone
who had worked with Cermak. Before his untimely death, he
was an Eastern European thug from Hungry, a communist
and an anarchist going by the name of Wota Klada. He'd arrested Klada a year earlier for being near the site of a dynamite blast. His alibi had stuck; he'd walked. Now he was worm

food. Another rumor had been floating around that pinpoint-
ed Klada to be telling stories out of school, to Cermak. The
coroner's van arrived just as Alfano was thinking that perhaps
hanging around with politicians in Chicago was an easy way to
either get rich, get beaten, or get shot dead and the unfortu-
nate Klada had ended up with the third option.

Alfano waved at the coroner's panel van on Washington,
it backed down the alley slowly but still almost ran over the
body.

"Couldn't you get any closer, bud? Where's the coroner?"

"…With a mess on Wells, two dead, a police shooting.
I already have one body in the back. Fuck, is that him that
smells?"

Alfano nodded.

"Shit, now the van will stink all day."

"…Too fucking bad, not my problem. I'll stop by and talk
with the coroner later." Alfano was on his way out of the alley
very quickly before the assistant coroner could yell, "Aren't
you going to help me with the body?"

# 3

ALFANO sat at his desk smoking and doodling on a note-book of lined yellow paper. Circles inside of circles, inside of circles, like interconnecting rings, like Chicago politics and vice, one inside the other, inside the other. Klada's file sat on his desk, all neat, nicely typed, a photo stuck in the upper left corner of the file showed the face of the dead man. Didn't look much different except for the dead part and the three days lying in the alley and the maggots. Jabrowski was right; the coroner had confirmed the approximate time of death as three days earlier based on body decomposition and the tell-tale maggots. *Ain't nature great?*

Death had found him with the help of three slugs, 45s, two in the lungs and one through the pump. Two slugs were found in the brick wall of the alley, one had remained in the body somehow. Klada's heart was shattered by the impact; he was dead in seconds. Alfano wondered what secrets Klada knew before his coup de grace. He had talked a lot about dynamite, bombs, taxis, unions and politicians, even about Cermak, a year ago. After Klada's attorney had come into the room he had stopped talking, two weeks later Alfano found out that he had walked after paying a $200 fine. *It's kinda funny, I remember, when I searched Klada, he'd only had a sawbuck in his wallet, but then again anything is possible.* Either way, nothing that Klada told Alfano was good enough for City Hall.

"Detective, can you talk with this woman? She says she'll talk to you and only you. Told her you were busy, she said that's okay, she could wait. That was an hour ago, I was hoping she'd leave. She didn't, just sat there waiting. So can you see here?"

"Give you a name, Sergeant?"

"Adele Doyle, lives on Taylor Street, her kid is missing."

"How old is the kid?"

"...Twenty-four."

"That's not a kid."

"Try telling her that."

"Where is she?"

"Room 1, I got her some coffee."

"That was nice, thanks."

As Alfano walked to Room 1, he tried to place Mrs. Doyle. It still hadn't hit him when he entered but when he saw her, it all came back to him. Mrs. Adele Doyle was an attractive woman in her mid-forties; a touch of the old country in her speech gave her an endearing quality. She had red hair, a thin build, her dress was fluffed out of the open collar of her black coat, she was clean but rough and a touch matronly. She also wore a cloth beret; its color matched her coat. *A few years ago, she was a looker, now she just looks tired.*

"How are you, Adele? You look good."

"Thanks, I don't see you at Jimmy's much."

"...Been staying away, me being a cop and all. Maybe I'll see you there after all this Prohibition blows away. How's Eddy?"

She paused for a few beats, then smoothed her hair, tucking a few strands under her hat and behind her left ear, "That's why I came to see you, Eddy's been gone for three days. Didn't say he was leaving or anything, he just didn't come home from his run with the Ace Taxi. No one's seen him."

"…When?"

"Last Sunday, we went to church, had lunch at Jimmy's. Then he left late in the afternoon to drive for the night. Ace had him on nights, I didn't like it, but he did."

"Didn't come home?"

"No, but he would have, I know he would, always came by in the morning to see me after driving all night. Has his own place, him being a young man and all."

Alfano looked at Doyle. *Been for five years since I saw her last.* "Did he have a girlfriend?"

"No, would have told me. No girls, he didn't have much money, but he gave me some to keep food in the house. Always said they were too much trouble and cost too much money to be around."

"He was in some union trouble, wasn't he?"

"That was all behind him. He'd gone real straight, worked nights. Ace Taxi is really upset; they sent someone around to ask this morning. He didn't return his cab from the last night he drove. I told them to shove off, they know more than me."

"Out for a joyride? Maybe headed up to Wisconsin or something."

"No, don't think so. All he said the last night he was home was he had a small job, he needed to help someone, booked him for a couple of hours, said he was going to give me twenty-five dollars if it worked out. Now he's gone and I could sure use the twenty-five, really could. No twenty-five, no Eddy."

"Wait here a minute." Alfano walked over to the police desk. "McDunnah, we get a report on stolen cabs in the last week?"

The sergeant rifled through the stack of papers on his desk, stopping halfway through the pile, he pulled out a sheet of yellow paper.

"Here it is…Ace Taxi, Randolf Street, reported a missing

cab on May 2nd, driver missing too. Edward Doyle was the hack. Was he her kid?"

"Yeah, thanks."

Alfano stood outside Room 1, thinking. He knew the kid; he'd sat in the same room his mother was in. He remembered the kid was an Irish hothead, always in a lot of trouble, especially with the miner's union. And he knew the kid had to drive a cab because he couldn't work in the mines down south. *Doing odd jobs for the union these days; since the arrest a year earlier, nothing had surfaced, at least nothing I knew of.*

"Mrs. Doyle, has Eddy been recently arrested?"

"No, he's a good boy. Has grown up, Steady Eddy they called him at Ace, always on time, always worked hard. Never no trouble."

"We'll look into it; the company also reported the cab missing. The cab number and the license plate are on our lists, something will turn up, I'm sure." Alfano wasn't all that sure, the cab could be in the Chicago River, or stripped, repainted and in Milwaukee. There were a hundred places a stolen cab could end up, most of them not good.

"You always been straight with me Tony; always could count on you for help. I'm asking again. Anything to help find my boy, I would be grateful." Adele Doyle reached for her handbag.

"How's Franky?" Alfano asked, looking at the gold band on Adele's left hand.

"He gets out next year, five years was too long for what he did. But he's better for it; saw him last month in Joliet."

"Good, he's lucky he didn't get convicted on that murder charge, real lucky."

"I prayed a lot, sometimes it works, thanks, Tony."

Adele Doyle buttoned up her coat and adjusted her black felt floppy hat. Her red hair stuck out at all angles under its rolled edge. She offered Alfano her hand; it was cold and thin.

*Yes, she could use that twenty-five bucks.*

At the end of his shift, Alfano drove one of the unmarked cars home, it was an impounded Packard, recovered from a brewery bust. The engine had been worked on, the mechanics in the garage said it had twice the horsepower now than it did when it rolled off the Detroit assembly line. He hated cars. They were expensive to fill with gas and expensive to maintain, forty-three years old and he'd never owned a car. There was always one available in the police garage that suited him.

"Good evening, Mrs. Kowalski," Alfano said as he climbed the second of three flights of stairs to his apartment, a paper bag under his arm. Mrs. Kowalski stood just behind her barely opened door.

"Good evening, Detective. I have some cabbage soup and good rye bread, interested?"

"Not tonight thanks, too tired, long day." Alfano stopped on the landing. Mrs. Kowalski took the opportunity to open the door. Alfano had to repress a smile. She stood there in a thin negligee, backlit by the soft lights in her room; there was very little left to the imagination.

"…Teddy home tonight?" Alfano inquired, knowing the answer.

"No, he's got the late shift at the mill, won't be back until 7:00 a.m. Fred Waring is on tonight, you want to listen?" She opened her legs wider beneath the sheer fabric, adjusting her hips slightly as she stood facing him. Alfano needed even less imagination now.

"…Can't, but thanks, as I said, long day and a longer one tomorrow." Alfano started up the stairs.

"Don't know what you're missing," she paused. "The soup's real good."

Alfano continued up the stairs, he heard her door close with a hard click. He unlocked his and set the dead bolt when he closed it. He sat the bag down on the short counter that made up half of the kitchen; he extracted a bottle of bourbon, a package of ground chuck, two potatoes, an onion and the *Sun-Times*. He turned the radio on; it sat on a shelf just above the kitchen sink. He heard the opening music of the *Sherlock Holmes* theme on WLS. As the show finished, his scramble of ground beef and potatoes was almost done, along with the first two fingers of bourbon; he poured two fingers more and sat down to eat dinner.

# 4

THE WELSH ACCENT carried like a soft tenor serenading a snake. "Careful lad, real careful, two more and we're good. This is your lucky day, laddie, your lucky day. I don't just let anyone watch my business, but I can see you have steady hands, cool hands. And I need to pass this on to someone; you're my apprentice. Yeah, real steady-like, that's it, good boy."

"Thank you, Mr. Smythe, thanks."

"Just pay attention, I've had apprentices before and none of them lasted. Got too fast or too full of shit, they found one fellow's head in the second-floor ceiling. It went straight up and through the ceiling above. He was good, but he was cocky. Cocky gets you dead."

Smythe pushed the thin pencil of metal into the end of one of the sticks of dynamite. It was secured to four others with black cloth tape. "I've had some luck with these Woolworth clocks, seem okay. Just keep' em next to the baby-girls; I'll attach the particulars when we're almost there, no need to test God's hand."

Timothy O'Toole took the taped bundle, Smythe's baby-girls he called them, and placed it comfortably in the shoe-box, the timer sat next to a small battery in the box. "Mr. Smythe, is three enough?"

"Two times enough, just want to make sure. The order was for front and back, at eleven o'clock tonight. There's a small trashcan out front and a coal chute door at the rear. At the right time, I'll place the one in front and you'll slide your box down the chute. It will look like I'm just putting trash in the can. You be careful. Slide it in, then walk away slow and deliberate-like. Got it?"

"Got it. I walk to the end of the street and you'll pick me up. We have five minutes after they're set. We'll be blocks away."

"That's my boy, six blocks. You park the cab at the end of the block, there's a hydrant there and they never ticket cabs there. We need ten minutes tops. You keep your box in the bag, like you're just home from work, check for eyes on you, then place the package in the chute and walk back to the car. I'll meet you there. Then we're gone." Smythe looked at his watch, "Two hours."

Smythe lit another cigarette and watched the setting sun reflect off the Chicago skyline through the high window, a purple haze developed behind the tallest buildings, a thin strip of coal smoke hung between the skyscrapers. In an hour it would be dark, in two, it would be just right. The saloon would be full. That's all he was told, make sure it's full. He didn't ask why, it wasn't any of his business. His business was dynamite and dollars, the more of one, the more of the other.

"Your mother, she good to you?"

"Yeah, as good as an alcoholic can be. But she's okay, the church helps her a little, I give her some money when I'm flush. So, she's okay. Why?"

"No reason, mothers are the most important part of life; they need to be treated with respect and honor. You do that for her?"

"That I do, Mr. Smythe. As she says, take care of those that can't take care of themselves."

"That's a good lad."

Two hours later, O'Toole pulled the Yellow Taxi to the side of the curb beneath a dead streetlight. Down the street, the neon flash of a vertical sign snapped on and off, an electric red arrow hung below, in counter-point, it flashed and pointed at the front door. Two men stood outside of Jimmy's questioning the patrons as they entered, Smythe watched them stop and talk with a couple that approached the door. Five seconds later, the man made some gestures and the two bouncers laughed, the couple turned and walked down the street, away from Jimmy's.

"Two lucky bastards," Smythe said, to no one in particular. "Damn lucky bastards."

Smythe took each box, opened it, and methodically went over everything, twisting and connecting wires. O'Toole held the flashlight. He slipped the first device into a paper bag and sat it on the floor of the cab. "Keep an eye out, that's a good lad." He did the same thing with O'Toole's package.

"Both are set for exactly eleven o'clock. There's only a ten-minute window, so get yours into the chute and then get out of there."

"Yes sir, but what about the third one?"

"A reserve my boy, just in case there's a problem. But these will work just fine." Smythe sat the third bomb in the foot well in front of the driver's seat. He checked his watch. "Ready?"

O'Toole nodded; he opened the driver's door. Smythe exited the right side, they both walked casually down the dark street toward Jimmy's. At the entry to the alley, O'Toole turned and headed toward the back door and the coal chute of the bar, Smythe continued on. Near the front door, he took a cigarette from his cigarette case and asked one of the mugs at the door for a light, the bag still held tightly under his arm.

"Evening gentlemen, sure is quiet."

"Yeah, just the way we like it," the big Italian said. "You

need a beer?"

"Not tonight, need to get home to the missus. She needs some help getting around these days."

"Stop by anytime, we serve the best beer in town."

"Sadly, I quit drinking a few years ago, but thanks for the light. You fellows have a good night. Mind if I throw this in the trash, some old shoes, just bought some new ones," Smythe said.

The two looked down and smiled at the black and white locally-made Florsheims.

"Smart-looking shoes," the big man said. "Yeah, go ahead. Have a good night."

"Thanks, I'm sure I will." Smythe looked at his watch again as he walked over to the trashcan, lifted the dented lid and placed the bag and shoe box just inside of the half-filled can. "Thanks."

Smythe continued walking down the street, away from the cab, slowly, counting to himself. At ninety, a thunderous ex-plosion lit the sky behind Jimmy's; Smythe continued walking without missing a step. At the count of 150, the trashcan in front of the bar exploded, scattering the bodies of the thirty or so patrons and the two bouncers that were tumbling out the front door trying to escape the explosion at the rear of the bar. Many were thrown into the street, some were thrown against the cars parked on the street, others were ripped apart by the dual explosions. At 200, the Yellow Cab parked under the dead streetlight exploded, the concussion blew the top off the water hydrant. The burning gasoline coursed down the gutter with the running water. The bulk of the taxi contin-ued to burn as the pillar of water arched through the Chicago night.

At 300, Davies extracted a key from his pocket and opened the door to his maroon Model B Ford. He pulled out a hand-kerchief quickly wiped the moisture from the side mirror and then he slid into the front seat. Once settled in, he removed his revolver from its shoulder holster and placed it on the seat; he took out his box of cigarettes, lit one, took a deep breath, started the car and slowly pulled out onto the dark street. The screams of the fire trucks began to rip the night apart.

# 5

TONY ALFANO was into his third two-finger glass of bourbon when he heard and felt the first explosion. He saw flames
twisting high over the roof of the building directly across the
street. Seconds later, another explosion, almost in line with the
first one, roared into the night, more flames were visible, even
faint screams echoed through the neighborhood as the fires
soared out of control. He downed the remaining bourbon and
slipped on his shoulder holster. As he reached for his coat, the
window rattled violently again as another explosion, this time
to his left, made it a threesome.

"God damn," was all he could say. Alfano quickly ran
down the stairs. Mrs. Kowalski stopped him in mid-step as he
reached her landing.

"What was that Tony, sounded real bad?"

"It is bad Alice, real bad. Stay inside."

Alfano continued pounding down the steps and out the
front door. He turned left heading toward the last explosion,
a tower of flames reached above the trees. Turning the corner, he saw the burning car and the hydrant gushing upward,
both pillars of fire and water probed the bare branches of the
trees, the stench of burning rubber and the sounds of fire
trucks began to fill the air. Running, Alfano passed the car

and dodged the falling water. At the next street, he turned and saw more flames and what could only be called hell's carnage. Bodies were strewn about the street and sidewalk; one car had caught on fire from the explosion, adding to the chaos, people were already gathering across the street.

Alfano turned down the alley behind Jimmy's and slowed down. His heart was pounding, smoking didn't help and the fact that he was slightly in the bag didn't help either. The fire roared, liquor-fueled blasts of flame from the back of the bar lit the buildings down the narrow canyon. The damage to the garages on the opposite side of the alley was intense, but none had caught on fire. Alfano drew his pistol without thinking and slowly walked toward the fire, he knew this was the site of the first explosion. The heat was intense. Halfway to the building, he saw a body; it was on its back, one leg wore a scuffed shoe, the other leg was missing. Smoke rose, steam-like, from the clothing. Identifying the body would be difficult; it didn't have hands or a head.

He walked down the alley; he saw nothing or anyone else. He watched as fire trucks and police cars arrived. He retraced his steps to the front of the bar; a nervous patrolman put his hand up.

"Halt, stop right there," the cop yelled.

"That's okay, Tommy, it's Alfano," he said as he recognized the patrolman.

"Detective Alfano, how'd you get here so fast?"

"I live a block away, heard the explosions. Like flies to shit, we are."

"Jesus, what the hell happened?" the patrolman said as the two men watched firemen and police trying to help anyone still alive. Weak arcs of water dribbled into the building, the nozzles on the fire hoses were wide open.

"Pressures way down," Alfano said. "The hydrant's blown on the corner; a car exploded down there and damaged the hydrant." He pointed down the street, the patrolman looked.

Ambulances and the coroner's van arrived; it would be hours before the fire was out. Men dragged the injured away from the intense heat; others had to be left where they lay. Six hours later, as the sun rose, the carnage became more evident, the houses on either side of Jimmy's were smashed in; they found four people inside them all dead. The coroner speculated that they had died from smoke inhalation after being knocked out. Fourteen were found dead on the street, twelve more were seriously injured. They may have found the remains of five more people inside the burned-out building. It would take time to confirm the actual body count. Much later, the body in the alley behind the bar was reunited with its mangled head—it was found half a block further up the alley. Alfano had been up for more than twenty-four hours when he was finally questioned about what he saw.

"Good God, Tony, that's a hell of a story," the captain said.

"Just another bombing of another illegal bar, half the patrons were from the neighborhood; Captain, this Prohibition is killing us."

"Don't I know it?"

Alfano knew it, he knew it for sure. He also knew that the Captain Frank Kennedy received monthly kickbacks from various bootleggers on the Westside, thugs that were not keen about the coming changes in the laws, new legislation that would make liquor legal. They justified their own bombings as business decisions to realign the sentiments of the other bar owners in town. During the last ten years, he had been to at least a hundred bombings in Chicago. But with the May Day bombs and Jimmy's, something else was going on. Someone was seriously escalating the butchery for some reason, a reason he didn't understand, yet.

"You're taking over the investigation, Tony," the captain

said. "That's directly from the commissioner and from down-town. Since Cermak's killing, city hall's been upside down. The new mayor wants you, but hell, he's just a political hack from the Sanitary District, Nash's next boy. But if we can't have safe taverns in this town, the public won't vote for him next time."

"I do what I'm told, Captain. But this one won't be easy; this may involve politicians, the Outfit. I'll even throw in a few guesses about the Commies and the unions. Frank, the rumors about Cermak were enough to have the feds all over this town and now with these bombings and the fair opening up at the end of the month, everything is fucking up in the air."

"Your job is to catch them, I want this stopped. Do what you need to do. That's the word from city hall. This isn't about the feds and Elliot Ness; we do this ourselves. Find this fuck-er, get it done."

# 6

TRAGICALLY, one of the dead patrons was Adele Doyle, her body was found just outside Jimmy's door; she had died instantly from the concussion of the second bomb. Alfano had pieced together a timeline, mostly from his own recollections. He used the blackboard in the squad room to map out the events: bomb one, the one in the alley, had exploded at 10:58 or near enough by his watch, the second exploded at 11:00, and the last, the Yellow cab, at 11:04. He guessed the alley explosion was set to blow, forcing the patrons out to the street, where they were caught by the second bomb. He still wasn't sure about the taxi, but he assumed it was the car used by the bomber and it was destroyed to mess up the evidence trail. He still wasn't sure about the mangled body in the alley, was it a vagrant in the wrong place at the wrong time or something else. He was leaning toward something else.

"There's a kid here to see you, said he's got something to tell."

"What? I got too much to do."

"Won't say, but he seems pretty upset, you want to see him?"

"How old, these kids seem older these days," he remembered Adele's twenty-four-year-old kid.

"...My guess, twelve or thirteen."

"Room 1, get him a pop."

Alfano walked into Room 1, the kid was sitting in a chair with a soda pop in his hand.

"That okay?"

"Great, thanks. Never seen you cops so friendly."

"That's one for us. I'm Detective Alfano; what's your name?"

"Johnny Cerjick."

"Well Johnny, the sergeant said you have something to tell me."

"...Maybe, not sure, all kind of spooky and all. We was hanging around a garage out on Lexington near the park, just checking things out like."

"I suspect you and your friends were casing the garage to see if there was anything of value there."

"Maybe, maybe not, as I said we was just looking around. Big lock on the door, wasn't there a week earlier."

"How did you know that?"

"It's our turf, we know everything," the kid said, puffing himself up.

"Sure you do, tough guy. So what did you do then?"

"Well, the lock was old, it kind of fell off."

"...With help?"

"Maybe, anyway we peeked inside and saw this cab, Ace Taxi on the door. And the place really stunk like something dead. So we backed out; I said to the boys, we should tell the police."

"Good boy."

"Not really, the others said I was full of shit, excuse me, didn't mean to say that."

"That's okay, I've heard it before."

"Like I said, we should tell the cops. The others said, go ahead just leave them out. So here I am."

"That's it?"

"That's it except the place was full of boxes of newspapers and paper. I took one, look here." Cerjick pulled a folded paper from his pocket, across the top, in bold letters, it said, WORKERS UNITE.

"May I keep this?"

"Sure, there must be thousands more in the garage."

Alfano took down the address, gave the kid another pop and called the sergeant. "Send a prowler to this address and have them check out the cab there, see if it's our missing hack. Tell them to be careful, there's a chance that Adele Ryan's son, Eddy, might be there as well."

"...Where?"

"My guess is in the trunk."

Alfano was wrong, not in the trunk, it was in the backseat and after four days it would take more than just replacing the seat to make the cab usable.

The sickly sweet stench of the dead filled the air, the unmistakable smell of horse piss and old wood completed the potpourri. Boxes were piled against the walls, all filled with flyers and handouts similar to the one the kid have given Alfano. Bundles of newspapers, all tied up nice and tight with twine, sat in the corners of the garage. They were copies of *The Nation*, the commie rag handed out at every demonstration and strike he'd ever been to. A quick glance told him that most of the copies were not six months old. The body was still in the backseat; the coroner was waiting in his van parked in the alley.

"Been a hard day, too damn busy, there are so many bodies from the bombing last night I had to use the hospital's morgue and it was a tight fit, and now this fella, any idea who he is?"

"Just a minute," Tony said, putting a handkerchief over his mouth, he patted the dead man's rump till he found a wallet. "His hack license says his name is Edward Doyle, the address is all here including his social security card. Too bad, Mrs.

Doyle never found out about her son, then again, maybe it's for the best."

"Why's that?"

"This fella's mother was found dead just outside of Jimmy's."

"Shit, that's just plain wrong."

The coroner walked to the other side of the car and opened the rear door; Eddy's head was buried in the seat. After a long look at the back of the kid's head, he said, "Looks like either a .38 or a .45. Close shot, hair was burnt some. Poor kid's face is a mess; probably a good thing his mother will never see him like this."

"Got a guess on time?"

"…Hard to say, no bugs. The car was closed up tight. But my best opinion is three, maybe four days, able to tell more when I get him back to the morgue. But he's going to have to wait, the mayor's on my ass about the bombing."

"Understand, your ass is not alone," Alfano said as he walked around the car, to the far side of the garage and a long workbench. Dust covered almost every surface, but it was disturbed in the middle, as if things had been pushed around and tidied up later. He pulled a cord dangling from a light bulb. The gloom of the late afternoon haze was brightened by the large bulb.

"Well, that's better," a voice boomed from inside the taxi.

Alfano looked down the rough planks of the surface of the workbench. *This could be thirty or forty years old.* Some tools were still stuck in a board attached to the studs, a rusty old saw hung on a 60-penny nail. Other odds and ends were stuck on spikes and pegs. Bits of bright objects caught his eye, wire pieces an inch long, others were longer, littered the surface of the workbench. Some were still wrapped in their cloth insulation. He picked up one of the longest strands. *Maybe twenty-four gauge, copper, electrical and bright. …Nothing this bright in the whole garage.*

He scraped together all the pieces of wire he could find and put them in an envelope that he had in his pocket. He found a box under the bench, a shoebox. It wasn't dusty, not even dirty; Florsheim on the end, size nine. ...*Small feet.* He opened the box, nothing inside. On the floor, he noticed a yellow receipt; Woolworth stamped across the top. The receipt said, in nice cursive script, 'clocks, six, $4.29 each,' the total cost was written on the bottom. ...*Interesting.*

He put the receipt in another envelope and walked around the garage inspecting the floor. The coroner popped his head up.

"By any chance, did you see a bullet casing in there?"

"No, is there one out there?"

"No, he might have picked it up, but my guess is he used a revolver not an automatic, cleaner, less chance of a jam."

"Likely, I'll know more later on." The coroner motioned to his assistant, the same fellow Alfano met in the alley when they picked up Klada. Ten minutes later, Eddy was transferred to the van, already the air in the garage had freshened a little.

Alfano looked on the floor again and noticed cigarette butts, at least eight. These were tossed there recently. Two had been crushed on the bench, he saw the smudges; the others had been extinguished with a boot or a shoe, one had a small bit of a label left. He put a few of the less damaged butts in an envelope, hoping they might be more than just paper and burnt tobacco.

He walked back to the alley and looked left and right, between the buildings the sun lit up the late afternoon skyline. He walked to the car and lit a cigarette; he put the items he'd found in a bag in the trunk and headed back to the station.

# 7

THE CAPTAIN SAID, "Downtown, 8:00 tomorrow morning, wear a clean suit," before Alfano could empty the evidence bag on his desk.

"...Why me? You go; you're the politician. Me, I'm just a Goomba from the neighborhood, Captain."

"I wasn't given a choice; the mayor and the police commissioner want *you* there. And our illustrious alderman will be there too."

"...Wonderful, three crooks in the same room and me without a reason to arrest them."

"I'd keep those cheap remarks to yourself if you know what's good for you. Just go and listen, play nice, don't piss on them or make them mad."

"Why should I? Chicago's a fool's paradise and they're the city's finest."

The captain headed back to his office. *Something must be up, that's the second time this week he came out and talked to me.* As a rule, Captain Kennedy never left his office except to go to lunch, take a piss or go home. Alfano was jake with the captain's way of running the station, never seen, never any trouble.

He dumped the contents of the first envelope on a clean sheet of paper, he counted the pieces of wire and flipping open his notebook he wrote: *ten pieces of wire with a cloth wrapping. Half of the strands are about three inches long, the others vary, but they're shorter. All sharply clipped at the ends with a wire snip, pinched clean. Good electrician, an expert.* Then he studied the store receipt. There were two big Woolworth's in the Loop, one on State Street and the other on Michigan Avenue. Checking the phone book, he stopped counting when he found forty more in the downtown area. These two would be his first stops; they were the biggest. Whoever bought the clocks probably bought their entire stock.

The shoebox also could have come from any number of stores. Alfano knew that Florsheim shoes were made in Chicago; the shoes on his feet were Florsheims. He'd call the Florsheim offices in the morning. Next, he dumped out the cigarette butts and looked closely at the ones that were the least damaged. At one burned edge, he saw what looked like the word PLAYERS, stamped in bold letters.

"McDunnah, you ever heard of a cigarette brand called PLAYERS?" Alfano asked the desk sergeant.

"Yeah, it's an English brand. Some of the fellows from the old country get them at the cigar store, special order. Some have them sent over to avoid the taxes. They're okay, not as good as Lucky Strikes, but to each his own."

Alfano looked at his notes and tried to picture the crime scene. He was certain that somebody assembled the bombs in the garage; someone who might have had new shoes, who used a clock from Woolworth's as a timer and was probably from Britain or maybe Ireland. The big question was which bombing were they used in? His first thought was the May Day bombs. That's about when Eddie Doyle was killed. *The May Day bombs did a lot of damage but didn't kill anyone. The bombs used last night were intentionally set to kill as many people as possible.* He was a few pieces of evidence closer to finding the son of a bitch who killed Eddy Doyle and probably his mother, but is there one bomber or two?

Alfano dreaded going up the stairs to his apartment. He

checked his mail, four pieces, and then unlocked the front door and slowly pushed it open. When the door shut tight, he was sure the click of the lock could be heard on the fourth floor. At the landing, Kowalski's door was shut; relieved, he started up the stairs.

"Tony, what the hell happened last night? The radio said that Jimmy's was bombed, twenty-four people killed - Tony, what the hell?" Mrs. Kowalski asked.

Caught in mid-step, Alfano froze. Alice Kowalski stood in the door, wrapped in a thick housecoat, her arms tight across her ample bosom, her eyes red. "Mrs. Kowalski, I can't talk about it; it's a police matter. Yes, people were killed, a lot from the neighborhood. I suggest you go see Father Polonius at Holy Innocents, talk with him. I'm sure there're many people over there praying right now." Alfano could feel his dinner getting cold under his arm.

"But it's all so scary, all the bombings. You never know whether it's safe to even walk down the street."

"Mrs. Kowalski, it's safe, just go about your normal day, you *will* be okay."

"You don't know that!"

"Yes I do, so stop worrying. Go to Holy Innocents; light a candle for the dead. Attend some of the funerals; it will make you feel better." He turned back and started up the stairs.

"You police are all crooks, for all I know some cop probably put the bombs in the bar." Mrs. Kowalski slammed the door.

"Shit."

After a dinner of spaghetti from Dominic's Italian Delicatessen and four fingers of bourbon, Anthony Alfano fell asleep in the large overstuffed chair that filled the corner of his small apartment.

8

AT 7:55 THE NEXT MORNING, Alfano parked the Packard at the Clark Street curb in front of City Hall. The signs said Police Parking Only, he wrote his name and badge number on a piece of paper and laid it on the dashboard. He slid his notebook into his suit coat pocket and headed to the mayor's office.

Three men stood in the reception area of Mayor Kelly's office, all three were smoking. His Honor's secretary sat at her desk, trying to wave away the smoke with a sheet of paper; she smiled when Alfano walked into the room.

"Five minutes, Detective Alfano, when he buzzes, I'll let you in."

"Thanks, Gini," Alfano said. The others turned toward him.

A tall man holding a cigar walked across the carpet and stuck his hand out, "Police Commissioner Hayden, Detective, heard good things about you."

Shaking the commissioner's hand, Alfano said, "Thanks, Commissioner, I try my best during these tough times."

"Yes tough times, they make people do things that they might not normally do."

"For some maybe, for others, they do what they want. Do

you know why I'm here? I'm in the middle of an investigation."

"The mayor will tell you, we won't take up too much of your time. Twenty-two years, how time has passed."

Alfano didn't care to remember the old days when Hayden and he were in the same Police Academy graduating class. Hayden was a rich kid from the north side, spent ten years wearing a badge. When Prohibition hit, he moved on and up to city hall as a dedicated public servant. His big townhouse, city car, and driver attested to his success as police commissioner and politician. Alfano also recalled seeing a photograph of Hayden and Capone shaking hands after a dinner party somewhere on the south side, Cicero maybe.

"Wife well?" Alfano asked.

"Yes, quite well, she's visiting her mother in Miami, been there a couple of months, the mother-in-law is not well."

"Give her my regards."

A buzzer sounded from Gini's desk. "He'll see you now."

Hayden led the way. Alfano didn't know the other men; one had the look of a soft meaty-fingered cop, the other was a thin-faced drawn man with an olive complexion. All he could think of was Laurel and Hardy.

Hayden looked at the men; they paused, then turned back and headed for chairs in the reception area. When Alfano entered the room, he watched as the door across the room closed quickly, the aroma of perfume hung in the air.

"Sit, sit, gentlemen, sit," Mayor Kelly said. "Detective, sit there, cigar?"

"Thanks, too early for me."

Kelly opened a large gilded cigar case on his desk, took two out and slipped them into Alfano's breast pocket. "... For later, Detective. Finding this bomber is critical for my city, critical."

Edward Joseph Kelly had been mayor less than a month

after taking over for interim mayor, Frank Corr. Kelly was mayor because a political boss, Patrick Nash, pushed for a special election by the city council that got his handpicked man the job. The assassination of Cermak changed the dynamics of the politics of Chicago, better for some, for others, worse. Kelly and Nash went way back; with Cermak gone, they were already on their way to setting up an unstoppable political machine.

"Detective," Kelly began, he didn't beat around the proverbial bush, "What is the latest with the investigation?"

Alfano looked at Hayden.

"Don't worry about Frank, he's okay. So where are you?"

Alfano pulled out his notebook, "Through a tip, we found the garage where we think the bombs were made, I can't tell if they were made there for the May Day bombing or the bar bombing or both. I'm following up my leads. The bombs were made of dynamite, probably with a cheap alarm clock timer. During the last fifteen years, there have been dozens of these bombs set off by the Outfit or the unions. There are a lot of people out there who know how to build 'em, too many people."

"Any reason why these targets were chosen?" the mayor continued. "A common thread, something they all had?"

"The five May Day bombs were dropped in front of big companies, important businesses. Easy to figure out that they were the target of unionists and anarchists. We were lucky there, late at night, no one about, no innocent bystanders, just the one guy injured, a night watchman. The bar was different; those bombs were intentionally set off to kill as many people as possible, all innocent bystanders as far as we can tell. That may have been mob work, to settle a score or something else. With the end of prohibition coming ..."

"That's not going to happen till the end of the year at the earliest, some beer and bad wine right now, we have time to get prepared. What's the bid deal?" Hayden chimed in.

"The president said as much in the newspaper so a lot of people are going to be out of work. I'm not sure it was a mob hit, if it was they crossed the line even for them. My guess is that something else is developing."

Kelly walked over to Alfano and put his hand on his shoulder, like a father would to a son. "I know you're doing your best, all the resources of the city are at your disposal, Detective. This son of a bitch blew up part of friend's buildings on May 1st, his was one of five. And do you know what else happened on May 1st, Detective."

Alfano looked at Kelly, thinking this had to be a trick question, "May Day?"

"No, it was my fucking birthday and this son of a bitch ruined it, I got calls from everyone, not one person said Happy Birthday. I was pissed and I still am. We need to show the world what a great city Chicago is. Anything you need, Detective, anything, you let me know."

Alfano, surprised by this piece of trivia, knew exactly where the Mayor was coming from, the Century of Progress World's Fair was opening in three weeks; the bombings might scare away the tourists. "Thank you, Mayor Kelly, any help would be appreciated, but you could have told me that on the phone."

"Don't be impertinent, Alfano," Hayden said.

Kelly looked at Hayden, "Frank, that's alright, the detective is right, I could have called him, but I wanted to meet him. You've worked under what, five mayors now?"

"Six, with you sir, it's been quite interesting."

"…True, true. Scandals, briberies, shootings, Capone, this Prohibition that no one wanted, and the assassination of my predecessor would test any city. But we're tough, we're stockyard tough. I know your record, I know you get results; that's what I want on this, results."

"Thanks."

"Do you want some breakfast? I'm having some brought in. Alderman Polk called in sick; he was supposed to be here, there's plenty."

Alfano's stomach growled in anticipation. "No, thank you, Mayor, I've got to get back to work."

"...You sure?"

"Yes, thank you, but no." Since the meeting was ending, Alfano stood.

"Detective, it's good to see that we still have men of integrity on the force, I'm not sure where this city would be without men like you."

"Thank you, Mayor, Commissioner Hayden." Alfano shook hands and headed to the door, it buzzed, then it opened. Alfano turned back toward the mayor, "Nifty gadget."

"Thanks, it's new, makes it tougher to get in. Good morning, Detective."

Alfano shut the door behind him; Hayden's two lap dogs were still sitting in the reception area. He walked over to Gini. "Those bums give you any trouble?" He asked, hooking his thumbs over his shoulder.

"Quiet as mice," Gini said, loud enough to be heard by the pair.

"More like rats," Alfano whispered. "This guy any better than the others you worked with?"

"Seems civil, nice to me, that friend of his, Nash, is in and out ten times a day, surprised he wasn't here today."

"It's good to see you."

"Don't be a stranger, call me sometime."

"I'll do that." Alfano tapped the back of Gini's hand gently and then retrieved his fedora from the table. As he walked out the door, he saluted Hayden's men, his fingers to the tip of his hat, "Gentlemen."

At the curb, a patrolman was writing a ticket; he started to place it through the windshield wiper.

"Jesus, didn't you read the note?"

The patrolman looked at Alfano, "Any slob could have put that note on their dash, who the hell are you?"

"Someone who just left a meeting with the Mayor and I'm not a slob. I'm a detective and I'm your fucking superior. Go up to his office; ask his secretary if I was there, I'll wait. Ask her about Tony Alfano. Or you can just tear that up."

"Jesus, Detective Alfano, don't get on my ass. I'm just doing my job; I walk this beat around City Hall, I get writer's cramp with all the tickets I write." The patrolman took the ticket and ripped it into four pieces. "... You happy now?"

"Yeah, as happy as sitting in a field of daisy's." Alfano climbed into the Packard and started the engine, it started with a roar.

"What do you have in that thing?"

"I haven't got a fucking clue, it gets me from here to there is all I care about." Alfano pulled away from the curb and headed back to his station.

Two hours and twenty phone calls later, he was certain that the clocks had been purchased from the State Street Woolworth's. Someone had bought their whole inventory of eight clocks three weeks earlier, the woman he talked to remembered the man.

"He was an older gentleman, well-dressed, said he was opening a motor court on the way to Rockford and the clocks were for the rooms. He was very pleasant. Why do you ask?"

"There's been a recent series of crimes dealing with stolen clocks, of all things, and I was assigned by my chief to follow up on them. But if he paid for them, he's not our man. But thank you all the same."

He hung up and added the information to his notebook; there was no reason the clerk needed to know more than what he told her.

He ran his finger down the cigar and cigarette store column in his phone book and found three shops on State Street
and four others in the area. *Maybe he's a creature of habit and shops
the same neighborhood.*

But none of the obvious shops in the Loop carried PLAY-
ERS. He expanded the area and after seven more calls, found
two shops on the near north side that ordered the brand from
a distributor in New York and one shop in the Drake Hotel
on Michigan Avenue. Maybe eight or ten buyers purchased the
brand from each. Five of the buyers were over fifty years old.
More pieces of the puzzle were found and added, more notes
were added to his notebook.

There was a large cork board on the wall behind Alfano's
desk; it hung next to the blackboard. He pulled a Chicago city
map out of his drawer and pinned it to the cork panel. He
wrote notes on small pieces of paper and pinned them to the
map. One for each bomb, one for each clue, the clocks and
the cigar stores; he hoped to see a pattern of pins materialize.

# 9

GARON DAVIES, known to everyone as James Smythe, slid the notice through the opening of the grill; the postal official slid his glasses to his nose, read it and disappeared. Two minutes later, he passed a package to Davies.

"Scribble your name here," the clerk said, pointing to the notice.

Davies did as directed and left with the small bundle under his arm, from the weight of the package, he felt confident that his client had fulfilled the next part of their agreement. It was his second package in less than a week.

The click of his two-tone shoes as they struck the wooden floor echoed off the metal panels of the ceiling.

A friend of his in the union had asked if he were still 'self-employed,' still doing consulting. Davies had known the man from his time in Denver so he had said, "Sometimes, but I pick the client."

"I don't know who they are, I just got a note. They knew things I was surprised about; in fact they knew more than I thought anyone knew. So they asked for someone with your skills, so maybe this time the client picks you."

"The Lord works in mysterious ways," Davies had answered. "I want ten large upfront and then I'll send on the information about the follow-up. Have them send me a note to this box number, I'll send them a reply. Then you're out of it. I'll pass on your usual finder's fee, will that work?"

"...Always."

That was almost four weeks earlier. The note had described the scope of the contract and the specified time frame. His first order of business had been to find Wota Klada.

Davies looked back at the line of clerk cages within the great hall of the main branch of the Chicago Post Office, straightened his fedora, reset his bow tie and opened the door. At the door, he lit a cigarette from a thin box with the image of a sailor on its face and went out into the rattling noise of the Lake Street "L" as it clattered overhead.

Davies really didn't care who was paying him; in fact, he was ambivalent. The money was good and it was untraceable. He was only a name on a cubbyhole at the post office, Smythe, with a Y. No first name. His contract with the unknown client established the required fees and the two operations had already put $30,000 in his pocket; the remaining four on the client's list would put another forty thousand. With the completion of the contract, there was to be a bonus of thirty thousand. He had two simple goals, make a cool hundred thousand and retire to California.

After changing cabs twice, taking the "L" for three stops and taking another taxi, he was close enough to walk to his apartment, a mid-block flat on Cortland. The walk also gave him the opportunity to see if he was being followed, no one could hide on the wide-open street if he were being tailed. He stopped at the corner store, bought some groceries and went to a basement speakeasy on Western Avenue to buy a bottle of Irish whiskey. He slipped the bottle of booze in with the groceries.

"Good afternoon, Mrs. Doolittle," Davies said to the woman retrieving her mail from the box in the apartment lobby. "…Pleasant day."

"…A right fine day it is, Mr. Smythe, quite fine. How is your back, better?" Mrs. Doolittle asked.

"Much better and thank you for asking, a little sleep and a nice walk does wonders. …Your boy, in school today?"

"Yes, he should be home at 3:00. All he talks about is the fair and summer vacation, I been saving up, few quarters here and there, we can have an excellent time. Do you have any laundry?"

"Thank you, yes I do. I will leave it in a bag outside my door later today, as usual."

"Thank you, Mr. Smythe; you are kind to me and my boy."

"Best I can do for the widow of a cop, shameful the way you were treated."

"Again, thank you, but since me and Charlie was only living together when he was killed, no benefits, so the road I made is my own. Thank you for the work."

"…Anytime, Mrs. Doolittle, anytime." He didn't know whether Doolittle was her real name or that of the dead cop, he really didn't care. *We all wear disguises to get through life.*

Davies unlocked the door to his apartment, put away the food and poured himself a glass of whiskey. Laid out on the work bench in his bedroom were three alarm clocks and a series of small panels with clips to hold batteries, a spool of wire and other miscellaneous tools. *So they want the bombs to have a different look, lots of ways to set-off the baby-girls, lots of ways. Lit fuse, mousetrap switch, cigarette, but a cheap alarm clock was the most reliable. And you could always carry the bloody thing in your hands and push the button yourself and see the face of your maker sooner than you might want to.*

He looked at the list; it was also used as a wrapper of the 200 bills in the envelope. This was what he liked, the weight of the bills, the heft, and the bills stacked one inch thick. The list was typewritten. The first name didn't surprise him and it would seem like retaliation, the other two names made complete sense to someone who was psychotic. Their deaths would only cause utter confusion and chaos. But then he was in the confusion and chaos business; anything to piss off the industrialists and the politicians was his motto. He was beginning to like this client. They didn't ask questions or make demands, they just sent him a list along with prompt payment, the list was typewritten, neat, efficient and organized. Davies was impressed. But he also knew they really didn't know Garon Davies; if they did know him, they would have been very afraid.

# 10

ALFANO READ the reports from the coroner. The kid in the car was definitely Eddy Doyle; he'd been shot in the back of the head with a .45 slug, it had stuck in the panel of the rear door. Some striations were left on the bullet; if they found a gun, they might be able to match it to the bullet. Almost no other forensic information was found other than the obvious hole in Eddy's head. He carried the usual information in his wallet, twelve dollars and a picture of Adele Doyle. He also had a box of Players Navy Cut cigarettes in his coat pocket; they matched the butts he'd found. Alfano was confused because Doyle's cigarette box was full, yet there had been eight butts on the floor. His rap sheet was not long, a few arrests for drunkenness and illegal union activities, nothing seriously criminal. He'd been a hack for a couple of years after coming back to Chicago from a coal mine in southern Illinois. The address on his license was the same as his mother's.

Sadly, there was very little information found in the cursory review of the dead and injured caught in the saloon bombing; all had died from either the fire or the concussion of the blasts. The body found in the alley was different, it had been shattered beyond recognition and even the fingers were gone. Pieces of the man littered the alley, yet the head remained intact. After it was cleaned and compared to mug shots, Alfano was not surprised to find the head belonged to one Timothy O'Toole, a small-time thug and bag man for a Westside gang. His rap sheet was twice the length of Doyle's and a lot more interesting. At one time, he had been employed by the city as a truck driver. Perhaps he was the bomber and one of his own packages blew him up? It would not have been the first time a bomber accidentally tasted the fruit of his trade. And if he wasn't the bomber, what had happened? The burnt blown-up car had actually been a taxi, a Yellow Cab assigned to O'Toole for the day; he obviously hadn't returned it at the end of his shift.

Alfano took out his notebook and drew a line down the middle of the next clear page. On the left side, he wrote the facts of the May Day bombing, on the right side, he listed those facts pertaining to the Jimmy's Bar explosion. When he was done, there were more matches than misses. Alfano turned to a new page and made some suppositions: *the same bomber made all the bombs, he was an expert with explosives, his presumed assistant died or was murdered during or after the bombs exploded, the assistants were all cab drivers and Irish, and there was no apparent political connection between the May Day targets and Jimmy's.* The last fact made Alfano's head spin because if these were arbitrary bombings, finding the next target would be a lucky guess, not a scientific deduction.

Alfano's phone began to ring; he answered it on the third ring.

"...Detective Alfano here."

"Tony, it was good to see you this morning, it has been a while."

Alfano took in a slow deep breath, "Too long, much too long, Gini. How's that husband of yours?"

There was a pause, "We split almost a year ago; he's on the coast somewhere."

"Which coast?"

"Don't know, don't care."

Alfano paused, he wanted to ask the obvious question about her personal life, but he set it aside, "How's the new mayor doing?"

"He's okay, a little like Mayor Cermak, bless his soul, having meetings all day long, some with businessmen, others with politicians from downstate and even a couple of people from Washington. Very busy, my days go by quickly."

"That's good."

"Yes," Gini paused again. "I need to see you, catch up on old times."

Alfano took another slow breath.

"Tony, did you hear me? It's important."

"How about dinner tonight, could use a night out, my apartment's becoming a jail cell. Yes, that's a good idea, how about dinner?"

"That will be fun, yes tonight then."

"You still live in that Chestnut Street Apartment?

"Yes."

"I'll pick you up at 8:00, Italian okay?"

"Didn't I always love Italian?"

Alfano paused again; did she just allude to the restaurant or to him? "It's a date."

"See you at eight, don't be late."

Alfano slipped the phone back onto its cradle; *it's been a long time since we played our word games together.* The last time he'd seen her was at the funeral of her boy, Tad, two years earlier. He had been five years old when he was run over by a sanitation truck. He had chased his new puppy into the street, the puppy lived, but the boy didn't. She was broken-hearted, the father had left them two years earlier; all he left her was the name Gale and the boy. Alfano had called for a month or two and thought he was helping. Out of the blue, she married an oaf of a German, why, Alfano never knew, not that he'd ever step up to the plate. He'd done that dance once, fifteen years earlier, it had lasted a year before she'd filed for abandonment; his only rebuttal had been: What cop couldn't be charged with abandonment? *Her call, what a nice surprise! Yes, what a really nice surprise.*

Gini was waiting just inside the glass door of her apartment building; light rain spattered the windshield of the Packard. Alfano, being the gentleman that he was, carried an umbrella to the door and escorted her to the car. Not a drop of rain touched her black coat.

As they headed west on Chestnut Street, Gini asked, "Our favorite?"

"I thought that would be nice, for old time's sake, haven't been there since," he paused, "since the last time with you."

She slid closer to Alfano and didn't reply.

The valet at Louie's Italian Restaurant opened the door for Gini and held an umbrella over her head as she exited and walked her to the door; Alfano met them at the door and tossed the keys to the attendant.

"Signore Alfano, thank you for the call, it has-a been too long," a gentleman in a dark double-breasted suit said as he extracted menus from a rack mounted on the entry podium. "May I take the lady's coat?"

"Yes, it has been much too long, Louie."

After returning from the checkroom, Louie said, "Please this a-way, I have the most excellent of tables for you."

They followed the maître d' through the restaurant, almost every table was full. A few of the men watched Gini as she swiveled her hips through the crowded room, most smiled if their dates weren't watching.

"It was a pleasant surprise to see you again this morning,"

Tony said as he placed his napkin on his lap. "...Been too long."

"You have this endearing habit of repeating yourself when distracted and yes, it's been way too long, it's mostly my fault. After I had married that lug, I knew I'd made a mistake, a bad one. I was embarrassed about it. At least he had the decency to leave; we were heading for a bad fall anyway. I knew it and he knew it. He got out before there was trouble."

"You okay?" He didn't bring up her boy, he would wait for her to do that and only if she wanted to talk about it.

"My ego is bruised, but I'm almost over that, and you? I see that you have the mayor's ear."

"...That good or bad?"

"Don't know yet, Kelly's a piece of work. The city council made it all official after Nash and his Cook Country machine helped Kelly win the election. Nash was in and out of Cermak's office more times than I can count over the last few years, now it's Kelly's turn at the machine, such as it is."

"Dirty?"

"Who knows, they all seem to get something from somewhere. Me, I just like my job."

They ordered dinner; the violinist serenaded them twice with Neapolitan songs. For the first time in five days, Alfano completely forgot about the bomber, he was looking forward to a long evening with Gini. As dessert was being served, an argument, a very loud and very Sicilian one, began in the far corner booth. Alfano could see both men clearly and he recognized the big man with his back against the wall.

"What the hell? I thought that thug was in a New York State prison?"

"...Who?" Gini asked as she turned toward the noise, which was getting louder.

"Sanartelli, a gangster from Detroit, I arrested him five or six years ago, he was extradited to New York for manslaughter."

"…Looks like he's not in prison now."

The yelling went up another notch. The two men were now standing, Louie quickly walked toward the two men, *"Signori, Signori, si prega di essere abbastanza, prega."*

"This is not good; when I tell you to duck, hit the floor."

Gini turned back and looked at Alfano. "Duck, why?"

Alfano watched Sanartelli reach inside his suit coat. "Fuck, Gini hit the floor."

She fell off her chair like a lead weight and flattened herself against the tile. Alfano stood and drew his automatic as Sanartelli pulled out a huge chrome pistol and pointed it at the man he was arguing with, he calmly pulled the trigger. The explosion deafened everyone within twenty feet; the man flew back into the booth from the impact of the bullet hitting his chest. Sanartelli pulled the trigger again, the man's inert form jerked from the second bullet's impact. Sanartelli turned toward the protesting restaurant owner and raised his pistol. A third explosion filled the restaurant. Patrons were either crowded under tables or rushing pell-mell toward the exit. Sanartelli looked across the room and saw Alfano; he recognized him right away and saw the smoking automatic in Alfano's hand. Two seconds later, Sanartelli ripped open his shirt with his left hand, blood was pouring from the hole in his undershirt. Two seconds after that, he collapsed to the tile, his heart had been ripped in two by a bullet from Tony Alfano's gun.

Alfano lowered his weapon slowly and quickly scanned the restaurant, not sure who else might be looking for trouble, a bodyguard or another thug. When there were no volunteers, he reached down and helped Gini stand up.

"You okay?"

"Jesus, Tony, what the hell was that all about?" She looked around the room; the smell of cordite filled the garlic-laden air.

"Old scores and current settlements, more than likely, the dead guy owed Sanartelli some money."

"And you, you had to shoot him?"

"Louie is a great restaurant owner, Sanartelli was going to shoot him and I was not going to let that happen."

"My hero, you sure know how to show a girl a good time."

By this time, half of the restaurant had cleared out; most of the customers probably didn't want to be there when the police arrived. Alfano walked over to the two dead gangsters, "You okay, Louie?"

"Si, I'm-a fine. But those two should not-a been here. The guy in the booth I grew up with-a him, not a bad Joe, been legit for years. I thought Sanartelli was-a gone to jail. I didn-a recognize him or I would not have-a let him in." Louie looked around the empty restaurant, "Damn, I'm-a gonna be short tonight."

Two hours later, the rain was still misting as Alfano drove Gini home, the wipers weren't too bad on the Packard. He offered to have one of the patrolmen drive her home, she answered, "Not a chance, this is the most exciting date I've had in years."

The questions and answers lasted an hour, the who, what, and why. All Alfano could do is answer the who. He'd left Louie a big tip. As they headed up brightly lit Michigan Avenue, he asked Gini, "What was it you wanted to talk to me about when you called me?"

She looked out the window at the wet sidewalks and glistening cars. "I heard something after you went into the meeting this morning, something I probably shouldn't have. It was from one of Hayden's mugs, the two guys that were sitting in the reception room. The heavier guy said it to the skinny guy."

"Laurel and Hardy?"

"…Who?" She ran her finger across the steamed window. "Yes, I get it. Yes, the Hardy fellow."

"What was it?"

"Just a phrase, he said 'He's on board, he's got his dough and the list.' The other one said, 'Can he make it work?' and the fat man said, 'No problem, two down, four to go.' I have no idea what it all meant, but they were talking while you were with the mayor. Sounded fishy, so I thought of you."

"Thanks, fishy, that's my line of work. Strange conversation, two down, four to go. Strange, and baseball has just started."

# 11

ALFANO WAS PISSED at himself for forgetting how great Gini was for his body and his soul. In the darkness, he lit another cigarette and offered it to her; she took a drag and ran her hand down his thigh ever so slowly. The electricity shot up his leg as if two live wires had touched him. "That feels good, don't stop."

"Don't worry, I won't, the night is still young and today is Saturday anyway."

They made love, slept, made love again. The thin curtains absorbed the early morning light and regained their pink color as the sun came up. He watched her tiptoe through the bedroom with a slight spring to her step, it made her breasts bounce.

"Stop right there," he ordered, "You are leaving the scene of a crime."

"And you sir are as much a perpetrator as I, so what's it going to be, crime or punishment?"

"Somehow punishment intrigues me."

"Keep that in mind and I'll be right back."

He heard her feet gently slap the oak floor of the hallway and then he heard the click of the bathroom door. The curtains breathed in and out, a soft May breeze wafted through the window. Her bedroom hadn't changed in almost four years since they had been apart. The pictures on the dresser were of a smiling boy, maybe five, bright eyes, dark hair cut straight across his forehead. There were no pictures of the men she'd known, either husband. No one would have known her past other than the boy; there were no pictures or reminders of anyone else.

She walked back into the room; Alfano had never seen a more stunning woman.

"You are beautiful."

"You are not too bad looking yourself, for a cop," she said as she crawled back into bed and laid her head on his chest.

"And you smell wonderful, too."

"You're too easy for a girl's ego. Hungry?"

"Are you offering another bite?"

"Right now, this girl's a little tired but hungry. Go take a quick shower; I'll wash up in the kitchen. There's a diner just up the street, the food's good. Some cops from the local precinct eat there. I know you have a lot to do, I made it a point to overhear what the mayor put on your plate."

"Are you spying on me? And besides, I really don't like discussing politics with a beautiful woman's breast in my hand."

She looked up at Alfano, "Well, maybe I'm not that tired."

After breakfast, he could still smell her as he drove to the station, when he rubbed his nose, when he lit a cigarette. Her scent was all over him and he liked it. *Too damn long, way too damn long.*

Gini Gale had put the flirt on him five or six years earlier, sometime after her first husband left her and the child's birth. They had met at a city hall reception; it had something to do with the then Mayor Bill Thompson's election run in 1927 and a publicized debate that Thompson had set up between two caged rats and himself. The outcome had been questioned; some believe the rats stole the show. "Big Bill," with the support of Capone, stole the election. Alfano had been surprised by her humor and warmth and the fact she did not take her employer, Mayor Bill Thompson, seriously. Alfano and Gini never discussed politics then, though she did say that Capone was the scariest man she'd ever met; she'd only met him twice and that was two times too often.

Their romance was warm and cool; she wanted more than he could give her at the time. He was on the city's gangland taskforce; it continually brought him into conflict with City Hall, Thompson and Capone's associates. He didn't have enough time to romance Gini and fight the mob. He was there to console her when her boy died, but she pushed him away and married the German shortly after that. Now she was back but their conversations drifted toward the cynical and suspicious. The boy's death had something to do with it, he was sure of that. She was still bubbly and full of smiles, but it all seemed a little forced.

"Glad to see I'm not the only one working today," Alfano said as he walked into the station.

"A few extra hours helps," Sergeant McDunnah said. "The captain offered me the time and I took it. My wife is with her sister in Gary for a few days."

"Did any more reports come in on the bombings?"

McDunnah held up a manila file, "From the coroner and the fire department."

Alfano took the envelopes and headed to his desk, he opened the coroner's first. The reports on the dead citizens at the bar were primarily of damaged organs and concussive deaths, some from flying debris and others from smoke inhalation. Eight were so badly burned that identification might take weeks if they were able to be identified. Alfano hoped that someday science would find a way to identify and decipher the clues of the mangled and burned dead. The fire department's preliminary reports of the bombings said that all three were dynamite related, used a timer, and were intended to scare, then kill, then cover-up the crime. The investigator was certain that the first bomb went off prematurely or was set to intentionally detonate before the other two. Alfano considered this for a moment and agreed; the bomber probably timed the detonation to kill the only witness, Timothy O'Toole. He was probably holding the bomb when it exploded. The fire department investigator interviewed one of the bouncers. Though severely injured he remembered seeing an older man put a shoebox in the trashcan outside the bar, the man had new black and white shoes. *Florsheims.*

Setting his coffee on his desk, Alfano opened the Saturday morning *Tribune* that someone on the night shift had left behind. It was the early morning first edition. The right column, with a bold header above the fold, called the investigation into the bombings an ongoing disaster, something that City Hall would like to make disappear. Alfano knew that the *Tribune* and the past mayors didn't get along. Alfano was sure that someone downtown, with the help of the Outfit, had put out a contract on Robert McCormick, the *Tribune's* owner and publisher. Noticing the lack of help he was getting from downtown, he was sure that the *Tribune's* story was probably more right than wrong. He turned the page to read the rest of the story. Prominently placed next to the final paragraphs was a short column about Alderman Immanuel Polk's speech to the Rotary. The lead read, *"We have become the laughing stock of America with our gangs, our politicians, and our elections. Not a day goes by that a new embarrassing revelation comes to our attention, and if someone speaks out, they are either run out of town or found dead in the Chicago River. In a few weeks, we will have a grand opportunity to change the world's opinion of our great city with the opening of the Century of Progress fair. Between the communists, anarchists, and the gangsters, this city has become a lawless town, like those of the old West, where the last man standing wins. I aim to put a stop to it."* Alfano read on. While he agreed with the alderman, he was also concerned about the general temperament of the speech; going public like that was dangerous in Chicago. *Jesus, I've become so paranoid that I am beginning to wonder if I can open my mouth about all the crap that's going on.*

# 12

DAVIES SAID, "Hold still, didn't I tell you not to move. This is the tricky part." The kid held the three sticks, bound together with black electricians tape. "When this is rotated, or even jiggled, the ball of mercury inside this glass tube will roll down to these two wires, complete the circuit and then these baby-girls get to dance. So don't wiggle them."

"Yes, Mr. Smythe," the kid answered. "Glad I can help. The boys at the Hall said it will help me get my card, all I want is my card. Then I can work at the fair, nothing better than that."

"That's a good lad. That fair will be something, all shiny and bright just like the future; I remember the one from '98, now that was something. Now, set it on the table and we'll do the next one."

There was no name on the list, just an address, one that Davies knew quite well. If there was to be a change in Chicago politics, it might come from this address, and Davies knew his client would not permit it. If a lesson is to be learned, use a big stick and Davies was very sure that six sticks of his baby-girls would do the trick. He was impressed with the logic and the list; each bomb had escalated a response. He had already heard that after the bar bombing, three men from a rival brewery were found dead. The *Tribune* speculated that their deaths were in retaliation for the bar bombing. The American Communist Party local headquarters denied having anything to do with the May Day bombs, no one believed them. Davies smiled at the thought, after tonight they would have even more to deny.

"Mr. Smythe, it is pure genius," the kid said, looking at the metal box. "And when the ice melts, the box will tip and the mercury will roll against the wires, we'll be miles away."

"That's the idea, Flynn; the box will be set against the wall of building, someplace out of sight. We'll put some trash and newspapers in front of it to hide it. With the temperature the way it is, it may take an hour, no rush, but in time it will explode."

"And if somebody discovers it and tries to pick it up?"

"It explodes early; very sensitive this package is, very reactive. Once it's set, even I wouldn't pick it up. What time is it?"

"Ten o'clock."

"We set the package at 12:00; it should do the job by 2:00. It's a warm night for May, so we should be right on schedule. Hand me my cigarettes."

Flynn picked up the box and handed it to Davies. He offered the boy one.

"No, cuts into my wind and I feel like shit afterward. Never really picked up the habit, my mother can barely breathe from her smoking so I stay away from them."

"Good boy, it's a nasty habit, but it does give this old soul some comfort. Had my first one while I was waiting for my da to come out of the hole in Wales, the foreman offered it to me as we waited to see if da had been killed by a collapse. Three cigs later, he walked out. Two months later, we were on our way to Pennsylvania, they were looking for miners, he thought it would be better there than Wales. He was wrong, it was worse. Those cigs were PLAYERS and that's been my brand since, reminds of that day every time I light up."

"Still bad for you."

"Agreed, but at my age, every day is a triumph. You'll never know when today will be your last day. Put that in the back of your taxi, I have an extra block of ice in the ice chest. Just before we leave, I'll cut it down to the right thickness, there's a blanket in there to wrap it in. You go to church with your mother, Flynn?"

"When I can, usually my sister takes her, they live just a few blocks from St. Patrick's; she has a car."

"Your sister has a car?"

"Actually it's her husband's, he's a cop. Good guy, been on the force maybe almost twenty years, out of the Racine Street station, a desk sergeant."

Davies took another drag and thought about the implications. According to the note that came with the payment, the detective assigned to the case was from Racine. He thought long and hard about whether to go through with the job or not; he could see no connection being made if the job were to continue.

"I'll put everything in the boot, lad," Davies said. "You make sure everything's up to snuff, don't want the police pulling us over for a bad taillight, do we?"

"Yes, Mr. Smythe, but I just went over it."

"Always check twice, good for business and for life."

As the boy busied himself with the taxi, Davies carried the steel box to the open trunk. He watched Flynn through the crack in the trunk door as he removed another small package from the metal tool chest and slid it to the back of the trunk under a small piece of carpet. Two bare wires, six inches apart, were just visible in the light from the streetlight. He wedged the ice block tightly between the tool chest and the side panel.

"Good here, laddie," Davies said as he gently closed the trunk until it locked. They rode in silence. Flynn, intent on the road and the stoplights, kept his speed well below the speed limit and he slowed at each intersection.

Alderman Polk's house sat on a tree-lined street on the near North Side. An alley split the residential block, garages and rear yard fences paralleled the alley's gravel paving. His limestone-faced home sat proudly mid-block and command-ed views north and south along North Maplewood Avenue. Alderman Polk had done well for himself and for his com-munity. Always a political animal, he didn't have aspirations of downtown and city hall, he was quite comfortable in his North Side fiefdom. He delivered votes as needed, found good city jobs for people in his ward, went to their funerals and retirements, and took vacations in Florida. His advice was sought and given, and seldom followed. It was also rumored that he was on the North Side mob's payroll; some said the rumor started in city hall.

Flynn drove north on Western Avenue and turned west on Division Street to Rockwell, then on to Maplewood.

"Drive north, I'll tell you when to turn," Davies said as he lit a cigarette.

"Yes, Mr. Smythe." Flynn cruised by the alderman's house slowly and then, at Davies' direction, turned at the next cross street.

"Turn down the alley, I'll tell you when to stop." They passed five garages; only one streetlight lit the center of the alley. "Go slow, stop now," Davies whispered. "Stay with the car, I'll be right back."

Davies pitched the cigarette butt to the ground, opened the trunk and reached into the back. He twisted the wires to-gether to the smaller second device hidden under the carpet. He secured the wet blanket and the block of ice under one arm and the lifted up the tool chest that held his baby-girls with his other hand. He walked between the garages toward Polk's rear stair. He'd been there two nights earlier to check out the area. Everything was still the same, an open area under the stairs, no dogs barking, the light burning in the high window of the house facing the alley located on the next street. The alderman's house was dark. He slid the block of ice under the bottom step, peeled away the blanket, and placed the steel toolbox on top of the ice slab. Only then did he open the lid and twist the wires together. He closed the lid gently and walked away.

Reaching the taxi, he walked up to Flynn, "I'm leaving you here, boy, you find your way home." Davies reached into his jacket and took out an envelope, "Should all be there, you be good to your mother and remember, if you see me again, you don't know me."

Flynn took the envelope and slid it into his coat pocket, "Yes, Mr. Smythe and thanks."

A flash of headlights from the far end of the alley, three blocks back, shot up the dark backstreet.

"Get moving, I'll walk," Davies turned quickly, walked between two garages and disappeared.

Flynn accelerated slowly and headed toward Potomac Avenue. As if on cue, the headlights behind him sprouted a red and white flasher on the prowler's roof, both cars gained speed. Flynn turned left on Rockwell. The police car spun out of the alley, they saw Flynn's taxi and hit the siren. Flynn pushed the accelerator to the floor, the cab's engine roared as he turned onto Division. The police gained on Flynn, at California he made a hard right again and came up on two wheels, just making the corner. When his tires slammed back onto the pavement, the back half of the taxi exploded into a scaring ball of gasoline-fueled flames. Flynn was impaled on the steering wheel, a piece of trim from the rear window embedded in the back of his skull, he died instantly. He felt nothing as the fire consumed his taxi. The force of the explosion rolled his taxi over and over and into Humboldt Park, it stopped when it smashed into an ancient elm tree just leafing out for spring. All the cops in the pursuing patrol car could do was look for injured people on the sidewalks and wait for the fire trucks.

Four blocks away, Davies heard the explosion, lit a cigarette, and stood next to his Model B Coupe, waiting. The faint sound of a fire truck echoed through the residential streets, he watched as two police cars flew by, heading toward the park. No one passed him on the street or the sidewalk; he flicked on his lighter, his watch read 1:33. He felt exposed; he'd waited too long, time to go. As he climbed into the car, three streets to the west, the sky flashed white, then yellow, then red, flames reached above the rooftops, then thunder rolled through the quiet streets. *Yes, it's definitely time to go.*

# 13

ALFANO PULLED to the curb half a block from the seared stone façade of the Polk home. Soot, in the shape of a black tepee, crowned every window. Glass crunched under his feet as he walked the fire hose covered sidewalk. He studied the adjacent houses and noticed that many had missing windows; luckily none of the homes were burned. The coroner's van sat directly in front of the burned-out shell of the Polk home, just waiting. Smoke still rose from the gutted home's interior.

"Alfano," he said to the patrolman standing at the door, holding up his badge. "Who's in charge?"

"Shelly, he's in back with the chief."

"…Coroner?"

"He's with them."

Alfano danced around the hoses that nearly filled the narrow gap between the gutted carcass and the singed house next door. Four men stood in the alley.

"Coroner, Chief, Detective Shelly, how many?" Alfano asked.

"Two," Shelly said. "Why are you up here, this is way out of your precinct?" The remark was edgy, overly protective.

"Orders from downtown, all the bombings go through me, 'till we sort them out. Not my call, sorry, Shelly."

"Fine by me, got enough on my plate as is. The two dead appear to be Alderman Polk and his wife; they have one kid at boarding school, the other lives in New York. We're trying to get a hold of them."

"…Positive IDs?"

"No, too badly burned," the coroner offered. "The explosion might have killed them before the fire, if so, they were lucky."

"Dying ain't lucky," Shelly said.

"Never is," the chief added. "Was fully engaged when we arrived, started back here. From the sound of it, had to be at least three or four sticks. Blew off the whole back of the building, shattered every window facing the alley, a few cuts on some of the nearby residents from broken glass, they were lucky."

"Except for the Polks," Alfano said.

"Yeah, except for them. One of our prowlers spotted a taxi in the alley about an hour before the explosion, chased the guy. He headed toward Humboldt Park, when he hit California, his taxi exploded, rolled into the park; it was burning like a chariot from hell."

"Really Shelly? How descriptive." Alfano commented.

"…Reading some detective trash right now, so the literary license is second nature."

"Leave it out of your report, okay?"

"Sure. When the cab fire was out, they found one body inside; taxi company said that a fellow named Tommy Flynn was the hack. He didn't answer calls this morning; we are chasing down anything else that shows up."

"Call me immediately if anything new turns up."

Alfano walked to the back of what was once a fine three-story Edwardian home; where a stair should have been, there was a three-foot hole. The rear of the detached garage had exploded inward; the Dodge inside it looked as if it had been in a head-on crash, no fire damage. The back half of the house was gone, the floors were now exposed and everything was nothing more than blackened cinders, the interior stairway was exposed and partially burnt. Two of the coroner's assistants were gingerly carrying a body on a stretcher; it was wrapped in a white sheet.

"They have the first body in the van, it looks like it might be a woman, we'll know more later on."

Alfano looked up and down the alley; he walked north for five houses, looking closely at the ground and the damaged cars. Some people stood in their backyards watching the investigation. He turned back to the three city employees.

"Shelly, don't move."

Shelly looked at Alfano, "Huh?"

"Don't move your foot." Alfano reached down, picked up a cigarette butt and looked at it, it was about an inch long, partially smoked, and surprisingly undamaged by all the chaos of the night. PLAYERS was stamped on the stub.

"Another piece," Alfano mumbled.

"What?" the chief asked.

"…Maybe another piece to the puzzle, the same brand of cigarette showed up at the first bombing, maybe a connection here."

"Every other Joe smokes, Alfano. What makes you think this one's connected?"

"Rare brand and English, when you got the habit, you stick with your brand, right? Well, if our bomber smoked Luck Strikes or Pall Malls, I would have less to go on, but these are special and hard to get, so may be a connection here."

"…Maybe."

"They move the car from the park?"

"Not yet, going to take a look?"

"It's on my way."

Alfano danced through the hoses one more time and

watched the men load what he assumed to be Alderman Polk into the van. *Yes, I hope the bomb killed them before the fire.*

There was nothing to see at the mangled burned-out wreck of the taxi, the body had already been pried out and taken away. Looking at what was left of the cab, the back half had blown apart, actually sheared off from the front, which was remarkably intact. All the gasoline was still in the tank in the rear. A man in a gray uniform stood near the scene, taking notes.

"You with the cab company?" Alfano asked as he showed his detective shield.

"Yes, insurance investigator. Got the call early this morning, this isn't far from the office so I came out and made a stop. Hell of a way to go."

"Never a pleasant one, the explosion probably killed him before the fire."

"…Probably. It was new."

"You mean the driver?"

"No, the cab, Plymouth, didn't even have 1000 miles on it. Probably get full value."

"Do you know if the driver had life insurance?"

"Doubt it, Thomas Flynn, if it was him driving, he was twenty-two, Chicago-born, lived with his mother."

"…She know?"

"Don't know, not my job."

On the ride back to the station, Alfano mulled over the jumble of facts and suppositions that bounced around in his head. There had to be a connection between the three bombings, something was tied to the cigarettes and the dynamite. His guess was that at least twenty-eight sticks of dynamite had been used, almost thirty pounds of the stuff created with the help of Mr. Nobel's imagination. This guy didn't buy it off the street, too easy to trail. Somewhere, someone was missing some dynamite, a whole box of it.

The desk sergeant was gone when Alfano entered the station; McDunnah never left the seat and his bad leg made getting around difficult. A patrolman sat in McDunnah's seat.

"Where's the Sarg?"

"Home, seems his wife got word that her brother has been killed in an explosion. McDunnah's trying to help."

"Her name wasn't Flynn, was it?"

"Yeah, Flynn was her maiden; Tommy Flynn was her kid brother, tough way to go."

"You have Sergeant McDunnah's address there?"

The patrolman rummaged through the desk and found an empty envelope with an address on it, "This might be it, seems right."

Alfano looked at the envelope, "Yeah, I think you're right. If the captain asks, I'm at a meeting."

"Okay."

Mayor Kelly was from Bridgeport, the Irish neighborhood near the south side of the city. McDunnah's house was located on Carpenter Street, a block from Saint Mary of Perpetual Help. The neighborhood was the Irish cultural and political heart of Chicago. The 11th Ward was as Irish as Dublin and, for some, just as radical.

Three police cars were parked in front of the three-story red brick faced McDunnah home, two uniforms stood on the sidewalk smoking cigarettes, both from Alfano's precinct.

"How's the family," Alfano asked the first patrolman.

"It's tough, seems the kid was killed in an explosion, they don't know more than that."

"The Sarg, is he in?"

"Yeah, he's with his wife and the priest from St. Mary's."

"Could you ask the sergeant to take a few minutes and talk with me, out here? It's important."

The second patrolman climbed the steps and disappeared. Two minutes later, he reappeared with Sergeant McDunnah.

"What's up, Tony?" McDunnah asked as he reached the sidewalk.

"Let's take a walk."

The two men walked up Carpenter to St. Mary's, then returned.

"Jesus, Mary, and Joseph," McDunnah said after he heard what Alfano knew about the crash. "You think Tommy might have been connected to the bombings?"

"Don't know, but this fellow, whoever he is, makes sure there are no witnesses, uses cab drivers and their cabs. Tommy might have gotten in over his head."

"He was always short tempered and anxious, at twenty-two, he'd already held maybe ten different jobs, couldn't last more than a month on a job before he'd move on. Thought that driving a hack would settle him down, seemed okay. Now this, what the fuck's happening, Tony, this isn't just getting close to home, now it's in the fucking living room."

"I'll keep you informed the best I can, you know that."

"I know, but if you find the son of a bitch, let me have him for five minutes. Then he's all yours."

"I'll see what I can do."

At the station, Alfano compared the cigarette butt with others he had, same brand, doubt they were from the same pack, but he was certain this was one solid fact in the case. The other came in a note on his desk.

"Did you put this here, Sean?" Alfano asked the patrolman manning the desk for McDunnah.

"…Yes, detective. The call came in from the state police in response to your request about dynamite thefts. A lieutenant asked you to call him."

"Thanks." He dialed.

"Lieutenant Symington."

"Alfano with Chicago police, the information you left with the desk sergeant said you might have some knowledge of stolen dynamite."

"Yes, and I heard there was another bombing last night, killed an alderman, damn shame."

"Yes, his wife too."

"Even worse. Yes, I might have some information. Apparently, last month, between April 15th and the 20th, almost two hundred pounds of dynamite went missing from the Thornton Limestone quarry."

"Why wasn't it reported earlier, been almost twenty days?"

"They didn't need it so no one noticed it was missing until they took an inventory, seems that four 50 pound crates are missing."

"Shit."

"I concur, that's a lot of power in the wrong hands."

"Can it be identified?"

"There are serial numbers on the crates and the sticks, hard to determine after they explode."

"Understandable, can you send me the information on the crates and the sticks?"

"Right away, find the bastards, too many dead already."

"Do my best, Lieutenant."

Alfano added the information about the stolen dynamite to his notebook. Then he recorded all the pertinent information about the Polk bombing, more facts, more mysteries, more questions than answers.

# 14

STEALING THE TAXI was easy. Davies was very familiar with the coffee shop; the early morning drivers always left their cars running when they went in for a cup of Joe. He'd cased the joint very carefully. When the time was right, he leaned against the corner wall of the alley, smoking his usual cigarette. He wanted one of the big cabs, a Plymouth or a Chrysler. The pickings were too easy.

He watched the driver leave the cab; the telltale smoke from the exhaust told him all he needed to know. He tossed his cigarette aside, stomped on it, casually walked to the driver's side door, opened it, slid into the seat, and, less than two seconds later, he was headed down Wabash Street going west. He took the cab directly to another garage he'd rented three blocks from his apartment. He drove around the block, watching for people on the street. At 5:00 a.m. there were few walking about, especially in the early morning rain. He pulled the car up to the garage, quickly lifted the cantilevered door and pulled the car inside. In less than ten seconds, the taxi had disappeared from the reality of the Chicago streets. It would take him two days to reconstruct the back seat, install the heavy steel deflectors and rig the twenty sticks of dynamite to direct their force more horizontal than vertical. He wanted the force of the explosion to be directed outward from the right side of the taxi into the face of the building.

After the Polk residence job, he was surprised by his next assignment, a corner commercial address, no second-story residential, all offices. When he walked past the address, he smiled. *Why the hell not, makes perfect sense, to someone.* The sign over the door read WARD 11, DEMOCRATIC PARTY. He had no issues with the party or its goals, hell, he even sympathized with most of them, but even he knew it was as corrupt today as it had been twenty years earlier.

He removed the rear seat and secured a heavy steel plate, shaped like the backstop for a baseball field, the two side wings would direct the force of the explosion back in on itself just for a moment, the rear panel would push it left and the majority of the energy would blow past the car door and into the building's glass masonry, windows, and door, through the room and then out the back of the building. There was a chance that the explosion would take down the whole building. The damage would be devastatingly newsworthy. All of this would take place in a fraction of a second and go unnoticed by anyone except an expert. Everyone else would believe it was the work of Republican businesses or their stooges, the Pinkertons.

Davies retrieved the client's next package from the Post Office, climbed back into his Ford and headed down State Street to a quiet restaurant next to the Grand Theater jazz club. Louis Armstrong's name was on the marquee.

"You ever see Armstrong play?" Davies asked the waitress.

"…Armstrong, who's that?" The cute blond replied as she looked out the window. Not many white faces walked State Street this far south.

"Louis Armstrong, from New Orleans, he's a trumpet player."

"…No, not my style. That's Negro music with all the shaking and hip dancing; no, too colored for me. I like a good Irish song or two with an earnest, respectful singer."

"Why am I not surprised."

"…About what?"

"Never mind, I wouldn't say Irish music too loud around here."

Davies mind drifted for a moment. *The money is good, another ten thousand put away for that sunny day looking out over the Pacific Ocean.*

Davies worked well into the night. The windows were blackened out with paint, he'd made sure every crack was sealed or blocked. During the two weeks prior to this job, he'd prepared the garage appropriately. The dynamite was held in a hidey-hole in the floor of the garage, a steel plate and lock secured his 'baby-girls' from potential thieves. He'd rigged the doors; they were well booby-trapped with trip wires and delays. He was more concerned about evidence being found than the carnage the remaining 150 pounds of dynamite would cause to the neighborhood. He meticulously pieced the steel together and welded the reinforcing plates in place; a cradle was built into the frame that would hold the ten 'girls.' Lastly, he altered the cab's exterior, a new name, a new hack number and a new license plate.

Every taxi company in Chicago, even those that were perpetually at war with each other, had posted a notice over the dispatch board, "*Report any problems with your cab to the office, by order of the Chicago Police Department.*" When Danny Flaherty phoned the office to tell them that his cab had been stolen, two things happened, he was fired and the dispatcher called the police. But someone in central dispatch screwed up. He posted every particular of the cab, a new yellow Checker cab, hack number 312 and its plate number. By mid-afternoon, the

information had been sent to every precinct in the metropol-
itan district. When Alfano saw the notice, he was pissed. The
plan was to gather as much information as possible without
alerting the bomber that they had made the connection to
the cab companies. Tony was sure the man had informants
inside, passing on gab about the cabs and their drivers, but
now he might proceed very carefully since the cat was out
of the bag. The last thing that Alfano wanted to happen was
anything similar to the "Taxi Wars" of three years earlier, a
lot of good men had died and many had been hurt. Nothing
would be gained by resurrecting the antagonism between the
cab companies. It was bad enough that they had called about
the stolen cab. Two years earlier, a cab had been stolen, within
three hours the cab had been found, the thief washed up on
the beach just beyond Navy Pier a week later.

The missing cab could have been taken for a joy ride; it
was early in the day. Maybe someone wanted to get home faster than the "L." But Alfano was fairly certain it was linked to
his case, his gut told him, that had been enough in the past.

Garon Davies parked his Ford on the street in front of
his apartment and watched Mrs. Doolittle walk up the street
while her son pushed his bike alongside her. She waved as she
approached.

"Good morning, Mrs. Doolittle, you too, Ralph. How are
you today?"

The boy looked at his mother then Davies, "I am very
well, thank you for asking, Mr. Smythe. And how are you?"

"I am very well, Ralph, very well. Mrs. Doolittle?"

"Back from the park, he just had to try out the bicycle and
thank you, Mr. Smythe. As I said, you needn't have done it."

"I never had one when I was a lad, it's a pleasure to watch
him ride it. What else can I do with my paycheck? I don't need

much, I'm happy here. And Ralph really needed a bike. Didn't you, Ralph?"

"Yes, I did, Mr. Smythe."

"How's school?"

"Hard, but I'm getting the hang of it, numbers and writing."

"You make your mother proud; she will need your help someday."

"I will." Ralph remounted his bike and sat uncomfortably in the seat.

"I'm going to the store later, do you need anything, Mr. Smythe?"

"Not today, I'm going out of town, sales trip down south near Springfield for a few days. But thank you."

"Watch this, Mother," Ralph said as he peddled heavily up the sidewalk.

"You be careful, you just started learning."

"Oh, mother." Just then Ralph slid over the curb and into the street; his bike tire caught in the wide openings in the street sewer grate and pitched him high into the air. He flew against the side of a car just as it was starting to accelerate at the stop sign. The bike was run over by the rear tire of the car; Ralph just missed having his foot crushed by the same tire. The driver slammed on his breaks.

Davies rushed to the boy; Mrs. Doolittle screamed and sobbed at the same time. Davies checked the boy. "He's hit his head; I'll take him to the hospital in my car. We can't wait; we have to go now. Hurry, Mrs. Doolittle, get in and hold the boy's head still."

Driving very fast through the neighborhood Davies watched over his shoulder for a police car. Luck was with him as he slid to a stop and carried Ralph into St. Elizabeth's hospital. A few minutes later, the boy regained consciousness and was talking with his mother. Meanwhile, Davies remained in the waiting room.

"Are you the grandfather?" one of the attending nuns asked.

"No, a friend, I was there when he fell."

"Can I have your name, please?"

Davies demurred, then said, "James Smythe."

"Thank you, Mr. Smythe, the boy seems to be doing fine. We would like to keep him overnight."

"You will have to ask his mother, Mrs. Doolittle. She will have to make that decision."

"She said she couldn't afford it and would have to take the boy home. We told her not to worry; we turn away no one. She said she wasn't a charity case."

"She's tough, lost her husband not long ago. I'll take care of the costs, just make the boy well."

"Thank you, Mr. Smythe, I'll tell Admissions."

Five minutes passed, Mrs. Doolittle came into the waiting room; tears coursed down her cheeks heavily. "Thank you, Mr. Smythe, thank you. You've been so kind. Now I know he'll be well, thank you again."

"You stay here and I'll stop by later."

"Don't worry, I'll walk home, it's not that far and I can use the fresh air."

As Davies walked down the hall, a nun approached and handed him a piece of paper, "Mr. Smythe, this is your receipt from Admissions, thank you for helping. Mrs. Doolittle is a very nice lady."

"Thank you, Sister, and yes, she is. Take care of her boy."

Davies walked to his car. *What the hell have I gotten myself into?* Davies lit a PLAYERS, casually laid the receipt on the seat and drove back to his apartment.

# 15

ALFANO PARKED the Packard directly in front of the stone façade of Gini Gale's apartment. She was only a few blocks away from the plush clubs on North Rush Street. While they beckoned with all their black jazz and dancing, he was intent on Gini's invitation, dinner. Life hadn't been kind to her, bad husbands and the death of her boy, yet now it had somehow pushed them back together. He wasn't sure why or for what purpose, he didn't believe in fate or kismet or much of anything for that matter. For a year or so after the boy's tragic accident, she wouldn't even answer the door when he stopped by; he could hear crying through the door.

It had been a city sanitation truck, no one was to blame, the puppy ran away from the boy, Gini was talking with a neighbor when she heard the brakes squeal, then nothing. Her world folded in on her and she was sucked into a black hole. She couldn't remember anything that happened for days after the accident. The hospital, the boy's funeral, the puppy being given away, visits by Alderman Polk and his condolences. There were drunken days and drunken nights, the hole seemed to grow deeper and deeper as weeks turned into months. But then the black slowly became gray. A woman at Jane Addams' Hull House spent days listening to Gini's grief, it helped

her come back to life. Through Alderman Polk, she got a job
downtown at city hall where her secretarial skills were valued.
She took some time to help at the Hull House and her life began to have meaning again. She learned to smile again.

He buzzed and heard the door's electric release; he quickly
climbed the three floors to her apartment. She waited at the
top of the stairs wearing a sweet spring dress; her hair held up
by a sparkling rhinestone comb, her makeup just right.

"Good evening, Detective."

He stopped three steps down, "You look wonderful."

"Why thank you sir, and the same to you. Can I fix you a
drink?"

"…Thought you would never ask."

The apartment was small; it was the best she could do after
Tad. She couldn't live in the old apartment, too many memories that continually nudged and poked her. The big German
lived downstairs and suddenly she was married, then suddenly,
she wasn't, then Otto, or Klaus, or whatever his name was, was
gone. He'd even taken the few dollars Gini had managed to
save. A rumor circulated that he'd gone back to Germany and
joined Hitler and the Nazi party. Alfano really didn't care, he
was just glad that Gini liked him again.

As he walked into the room, with its threadbare beige carpet and thick curtains, he was pleasantly surprised by a vase of
flowers on the low oval table placed near the couch. A cigarette case sat next to the light blue and pink bouquet.

"Aren't those pretty, they're sweet peas, early, the florist
said they came up from down south on the train this morning.
Fresh and delightful, aren't they?"

"Nice."

"You are so creative, nice? All you can say is nice?"

"They are the prettiest flowers I've ever seen."

"Now you're just boring. …Drink?"

"…Waiting."

"Here." She handed him a tall glass with ice and a concoction of yellow liquid and fruit pieces.

"What is this?"

"It is called a margarita, quite nice, it's made with hard-to-get tequila, lemon juice, and some other things. The day is so nice, I thought that something fun was in order."

He tapped his glass to hers. "Did you have to go in today?"

"No, I was able to get the day off and tomorrow off as well."

"Tomorrow is Sunday and it's Mother's Day." As soon as he said it, he'd wished he could take it back. "Sorry."

"Don't worry about me, I'm fine. I'll keep myself very busy tomorrow; this apartment certainly needs a good cleaning and Tad is always with me, in my heart."

"Should I come over, maybe help you."

"I don't think you know which end of a broom works the best. So, thank you but no, I will be very busy and you, Detective Alfano, would only be in the way."

"I like being in the way but there's too much going on anyway."

Dinner was traditional Italian and about as good as Sunday meals at his mother's long-ago.

"I have to admit, the sauce is from the deli up the street and so is the bread and all the other fixings, but I did cook the pasta and light the candles."

"All wonderful, your Chianti selection was perfect, my compliments to the chef and chief candle lighter."

"Thank you, Detective." She poured more wine. "Funny thing happened yesterday in the mayor's office."

"You probably shouldn't tell me about it then if it was funny."

"Not funny like ha, ha, but funny like why, why. He called me in and pointed to the painting of Roosevelt; it was the one that Mayor Cermak put up."

"I remember the painting, not a photo, a real painting."

"That's the one, well it was sitting on the floor, leaning against a chair, there was a safe where it once hung."

"Maybe you shouldn't tell me, remember, I'm a cop."

"I know, but I'm telling you because you'll hear about it eventually. Well, the Mayor asked me if I knew the combination. I said no, in fact, I didn't even know there was a safe behind Mr. Roosevelt. I told him it was probably Mayor Cermak's and that only he knew what it was for and why it was there. Kelly's only been mayor for four weeks and is still learning the layout of the office. He said he was looking around and spotted the safe hidden behind the president."

"Probably, Cermak certainly had secrets and I'm sure a whole bunch went with him to the grave."

"Well, Mayor Kelly was intrigued so he called a safe cracker to come in and try to open the thing. About this time, Mr. Nash walked in; even he was surprised by the safe. So Cermak even kept secrets from his political patron, it was all very strange. This little man comes in and walks directly into the mayor's office, never even said hello. My guess is the mayor and the fellow have a history. Twenty minutes later, I hear, 'I'll be damned,' come out of the office. Curious, I stuck my head in the open door."

"'You sure you don't know what was in this safe, Gini?' Nash asked. 'Positive sir,' I answered. Well, it turns out, it was empty, 'Empty as a banker's heart,' was what Kelly said. Surprised me, I tell you. Why have a safe if you have nothing in it."

"After Cermak's death, did anyone spend some time in there alone?"

"No, not even when Corr was the temporary mayor. I would have heard, all too strange. What happens at night with the cleaning crew, well that's something else again."

"I agree, Cermak was rumored to have friends in less than

honorable places, but then again, there isn't a politician in this town that can claim virginity when it comes to the Outfit and big money."

"The safe has a new combination that only Kelly and Nash know and the president is back on the wall."

"Nice to have a private safe in your office, you never know when one of those things might come in handy, a nice place to conveniently hide something from someone."

"You've become a cynic."

"Become?"

"Yes, or at least a lot more cynical than in the old days."

"They were good days then."

"Yes, they were, before the pain and loss."

"Sorry, didn't mean to say anything."

"That's okay."

"Do you want me to stay?"

"Yes, that would be nice."

# 16

MRS. DOOLITTLE SAID, "What a wonderful Mother's Day present," to Davies as she held her son in the front room of their apartment. "He's well, that's all I could ever ask for."

"How are you feeling, big boy?"

"I'm better, thank you, Mr. Smythe, thank you for taking me to the hospital. I'm sorry about the bicycle. Really I am."

"Why don't you go take a look in the backyard?"

Ralph looked at his mother, she was looking at Davies. "What have you done?"

"The boy will tell you." He watched Ralph run to the back door.

"It's a new bike, Mother, he bought me a new bike," echoed down the long hallway.

"You shouldn't have, Mr. Smythe. Really, you should not have done that."

"Mother's Day is best spent with a happy child, so have a great day."

"I thought you had to head downstate?"

"I leave later this afternoon, we have meetings tomorrow and I want a head start. Never a day of rest in my line of work."

"You never told me what you do?"

"…A little of this and a little of that, mostly sales, farm equipment and conveyors, nothing special."

"Aren't you getting a little old for all that?"

"Age is about how you feel and I feel great."

Ralph walked into the small parlor, stood directly in front of Davies and put his small hand out, "Thank you, Mr. Smythe, thank you very, very much. And I promise not to break this one."

"I know you won't, I'll be gone for a few days. You take care of your mother; will you do that for me?"

"Yes, sir."


Two hours later, Garon Davies parked his Ford Coupe a few blocks off South Halsted Street, in the Irish neighborhood of Bridgeport, near Nativity of Our Lord Church. He walked two blocks back to Halsted and hailed a cab, he went north. He had the driver drop him at the Lake Street "L," he over-tipped him, an Irishman about fifty, and thanked him for a pleasant ride. Then he rode the train to within three blocks of his apartment. It was getting dark. He stopped at a speakeasy and downed a glass of whiskey, "For courage," he announced.

"James Smythe, my man, why courage?" the bartender asked.

"Paddy, these days, everything we do is for courage."

The bartender smiled and went back to cleaning glasses. At 10 p.m., Davies walked to the garage, changed into typical cab driver attire, put on a cap he'd saved from Eddy Doyle, backed the altered taxi out into the alley, closed the garage door and headed south.

He drove south along South Michigan Avenue, past Roosevelt Road. On the east side of the broad tree-lined avenue, the dark waters of Lake Michigan created the backdrop for the bright lights that blazed over the construction site of the Century of Progress Fair. He turned east onto Cermak Road, renamed for Mayor Cermak, and headed toward the 22nd Street entry to the fair. His taxi was like dozens of others cruising around the edges of the fair, their drivers wondering what lay in store for them the rest of the summer. How many tourists would come? How many would need a ride? How much money would they make?

Davies took it all in, the main entry done in grand style, the lights, trucks still arriving and exiting, trying to make the opening deadline; it was less than two weeks away. He took note of the panel trucks that passed him by, wrote down their names and the phone numbers painted on their side panels. During the next half hour, he recorded five names that looked promising. Davies backtracked to Roosevelt Road and headed west, then south on Halsted Street into the meatpacking district and Bridgeport, the Irish neighborhood. He drove past his coupe, grateful that it looked untouched. Two blocks further down, he parked the taxi on the corner of 37th Street and Halsted. A brick building stood immediately to his right, on the northeast corner. WARD 11 DEMOCRATIC PARTY was neatly carved in stone at the top of the building. It was 11:30 p.m.

As he walked back to his coupe, he hummed a Welsh tune he'd learned from his father almost fifty-years earlier, a ballad about miners, their sins, and their '*Hiraeth*,' homesickness. He lit a PLAYERS. As he approached his car, two young men stepped out of the shadows near the church.

"What are ya humming, old man? Sounds like a bit of Ireland," the taller man said, his red hair flashing in the overhead streetlight.

"Tah, that it might be. But laddies, it's from Wales, Celtic to be sure, but not Irish."

"And what is your lordship doing out this late at night, you a hack?"

"Yes, me boy, that I am. But I'm going home now. So if you'd excuse me."

"Me and Mikey are wondering what a man like you, and we know everyone here, would be doing in our neighborhood this late at night, especially on a Sunday."

"Lad, please, no trouble now. I've got to get home to my missus."

"Mikey, there's a toll here in Bridgeport, isn't there?"

"By God, you're right, Tommy, there most certainly is."

"See your lordship, a toll must be paid."

"I really don't think so, my missus needs every dollar I make."

"Too fucking bad, the toll is fifty."

Davies looked at his watch.

"The lordship has a train to catch?"

"Something like that," Davies turned away from the two men and started to walk toward his Ford coupe.

"Where the fuck you going?"

"...Home."

The flash illuminated the street a half second before the explosion knocked the two boys to the ground. Davies had just enough time to slip between two buildings, the concussion washed by him. He stepped back out onto the sidewalk, dropped his cigarette, removed the revolver from his pocket and walked up to the two men. They were still rolling around on the pavement.

"Sorry, boys," Davies fired one bullet through each man's head.

Seconds later, he was in his car heading to 35th Street, then east, past White Sox Ball Park and north onto Michigan Avenue. Fifteen minutes later, he parked his coupe in front of the Drake Hotel, handed a sizable tip to the valet and returned to the room he had booked the previous day. *The shower will feel good.*

Alfano was asleep when the call came in.

"Where?" was the first thing he said, not hello, not who the fuck is there. It was as if he knew. Ten minutes later, he was heading south on Western Avenue toward the Back of the Yards and Bridgeport. Cutting east on 35th Street, he could tell where he was from the smell; the Union Stock Yards flew past on his right as he approached Halsted. He waited as two fire trucks raced past, he pulled in behind them. Just ahead, five more trucks, lights flashing, blocked the street. He pulled to the curb, put his hat on his head and walked to the fire that still burned furiously fueled by the contents of the 11th Ward building. Most of the south wall had been crushed, collapsed inward. The explosive force had pushed what was left of what looked like a cab into the side of the building directly across from his 37th Street location. Alfano saw that the hole in the street was shallow; there was a horizontal pattern carved across the pavement toward the destroyed building.

"There will be some very pissed-off people when the news breaks," Alfano said to the precinct sergeant, he had just arrived. His uniform set him apart from the heavily garbed firemen. Two patrolmen followed their sergeant like trained dogs.

"That's a God-assured judgment," the cop said, his Irish brogue hard and rough. "There will be hell to pay. And who the bloody hell are you, governor?"

"Detective Alfano, Sgt. Racine, here at the request of the mayor."

"Well good for you. He's going to be one of those pissed-off people, he grew up less than five blocks from here."

"Sergeant," another patrolman said as he walked up to Alfano and the sergeant. "You need to see this."

"What?"

"I've got two men down a block and half from here—that way." The cop pointed east on 37th. "From the looks of it, they've both been shot."

"…Dead?"

"Very."

"Lead on."

The five men walked down 37th. The fire began to die down; searchlights from the fire trucks washed the scene. People lined the far side of the street two and three deep, children stood to the front, some still in their pajamas. Most of the onlookers had relatives either on the fire trucks or in the police force. To many, the bombing of the 11th Ward building was as bad as bombing a church. When Alfano reached the men crumpled on the sidewalk, he washed his flashlight over the bodies. Each lay face up; one hole in each of their foreheads. Both faces wore an expression of surprise and shock.

"Do any of you fellows recognize them?" Alfano asked.

"That's Tommy Malloy on the left, lives two blocks from here, minor stuff, bit of a delinquent past, maybe twenty years old," one of the patrolmen offered. "The other is his cousin, Michael Malloy, maybe nineteen, thick they were. Always together, their uncle is a cop."

"Shitty way to die," the sergeant said.

"Is there an unshitty way to die, Sergeant?" Alfano said as he began to look around the bodies. "See any casings about?" When he heard no reply, he wasn't surprised. Same as the other killings, the shooter used a revolver. As he pointed the flashlight further up the sidewalk, a flash of white caught in the beam. "There you are, you bastard."

"What is it?"

"Just a bit of evidence that ties this to the other bombings." Alfano picked up the cigarette butt and put the light on it. Half burned, PLAYERS as big as a billboard, written on the side. The man hadn't even crushed it.

They marched back to the fire. The Fire Chief walked over to Alfano. "I really hate this son of a bitch, the building was empty or at least that's what the alderman says, he's over there. This one was big, Alfano, two or three times bigger than his others, maybe twenty sticks of dynamite. If his goal was to level the building, he did a devil's job of it."

"Sergeant, have your men ask around; see if anyone saw anything or anyone just before the explosion. If the Malloy boys were out on the streets, maybe there were others," Alfano said as he walked over to the smoking taxi. One whole side had been blasted away, the opposite side, the driver's side, remained relatively intact even though it had been crushed by the impact of the building as it was propelled across 37th Street. The fire inspector, the same one from the Polk residence explosion, was standing off to the side, making notes about the cab.

"What do you think?"

"What's missing?"

Alfano looked closely at the wreckage, "No back seat."

"You win the big cigar; saw this in the war, the dynamite was directed to one side, instead of radially as it would normally explode. He built something into the backseat that forced the explosion toward the building; all it took was a little guidance. This guy is good, damn good."

"My thinking is that he's an experienced demolitions man, correct?"

"It's a good bet. He's done it three different ways now, each to the full effect, considering what he needed to accomplish. I'm sure a timer was also used here. He was either heading away or was long gone when it went off."

"I found two dead men over there, both shot," Alfano added. "They probably saw the man or talked to him. He leaves no witnesses. Jesus, he's a hard bastard. Four days ago, there was a report of a stolen taxi; this one matches the model. My guess is the taxi number and plates have been changed."

The Fire Chief walked over to Alfano, "This just came

over the radio, Mayor Kelly is on his way."

"You have a radio?"

"New, just installed in my car, a lot faster than a call box when you can find one that still works."

"Great, the Mayor, just what I need!" Alfano lit a cigarette; he wished he could get a drink. He couldn't remember the last time he'd had a good night's sleep, Gini's face flashed by.

# 17

MAYOR EDWARD JOSEPH KELLY, a scion of Bridgeport, was one very pissed-off Irishman. When his limousine rolled to a stop just outside the tangle of fire trucks and fire hoses, the first man he headed toward was Anthony Alfano.

*I guess now's not the best time to ask for a promotion.*

"Alfano, they have hit my house, they have struck at my heart and the heart of my people!" Kelly yelled. "I grew up here, I played here as a kid, I worked the polls from this building, my sweat dripped on its tile floors during long hot summers and now some asshole has the fucking gall to attack it. You have five days to find this fucker; I want him caught, or worse. Do you hear me?"

Alfano would have to be stone deaf not to have heard him. In fact, most of Bridgeport heard their current favorite son berate Alfano. But not one person clapped or said anything; they were as stunned as the mayor by the audacity of the bombing.

"I'm closer, a lot closer to finding him."

"Unless you have your hand in his fucking shorts, I don't want to hear about it."

Alfano saw another car's headlights light up the mayor's car.

Police Commissioner Hayden wove his way through the tangle to his boss and Alfano.

"Well, Tony, you've got a shit-bag full of nothing now."

"Thanks for the support, Commissioner."

"What are you doing here, Hayden? This isn't your neighborhood."

"I was coming home from an engagement when I was told about the explosion, got here as fast as possible. Sorry Mayor, I know how much this building meant to you."

"Thanks, Hayden. Alfano was trying to tell me he has his hands around this bomber's fucking privates, weren't you, Tony?"

Alfano looked at the pair; they looked like they were jackals salivating over a wounded goat. "Yes, Commissioner, the Mayor was just telling me that he will give me all the department support I need to find this guy."

The mayor's eyes shot bullets at Alfano, but he couldn't say anything.

Hayden looked at the smoking building, "Excellent. I'll see what I can do to help as well. Mayor, I offer my sincere condolences."

"Alfano, I want to see you and Hayden in my office at ten sharp tomorrow morning. And don't be late." Alfano wanted to come back with a smart remark but thought better of it. Hayden shook his head in agreement and left.

Mayor Kelly and Alfano watched Hayden walk back to his car.

"Don't ever fuck with me like that again, Alfano, you rely too much on my generosity."

"I do and thanks. Sorry, but the commissioner and I have issues, your help smooths out the road. Thanks again, I apologize and I won't be late."

The mayor turned and headed toward a group of men who were standing on the curb on the opposite side of the street. Alfano recognized Ward 11's alderman. Two patrolmen walked past the mayor, saluted, then headed directly to Alfano.

"What'd you find?"

"A kid knew the Malloys, he was with them until 11:45 or so, they left the bar and headed up 37th. He waited at Halsted, he saw them stop and talk to a man who had just parked a taxi. He didn't pay it any mind. He turned and walked the other way. When the explosion happened, he was two blocks away. When he ran back, he didn't see anybody, just smoke and fire."

"Did he see the man from the taxi?"

"Yes, described him as older, dressed in a hack outfit and a cap. Walked fast, sharply, nothing special. Was a white guy, he saw him when he lit a cigarette."

"He didn't see him leave?"

"He's not sure. When he reached the fire, he saw a car's headlights flick on over near the church parked under a street light, then it drove away."

"Did he recognize the car?"

"Yeah, it was a new bitchin' Model B Ford Coupe, 'wish I had me one,' was what he said."

"Thanks."

Alfano stopped at an all-night diner on South State Street. The place was full from the late night crowd that had just left the jazz club three buildings up the street. He ordered eggs, hash, and coffee. His day had started four hours earlier than usual and there was a lot of day left.


Sergeant McDunnah was at his desk when Alfano entered the station.

"The mayor called, wanted to know where you were."

"I was having breakfast; getting waked up in the middle of the night makes me hungry."

"Hey, don't get all over me; I'm just your answering service."

"Sorry, Sarg, all this is shit. No pattern, no M.O., nothing that links one bombing to the next, except for a stupid cigarette butt. How's your wife?"

"Coping, I told her she didn't need to identify the body; I'd take care of it. Wouldn't have nothing to do with it, we went together yesterday afternoon. The bastard who did this will pay, that's for damn sure."

"How many Ford Coupes have you seen about?"

"...New ones?"

"...Yeah."

"They are rare and expensive, cost maybe five or six hundred, some guys will pay a premium. For most people, it's a third of their yearly take-home pay."

"Guy would have to be fixed."

"Or work for the Outfit or have some other source of money."

"Can you do a trace for me? Find out from the state if any new 1933 Model B Coupes have been sold in the Chicago area."

"Was there a color?"

"Shit, forgot to ask, they been black so long I forgot."

"As soon as motor vehicles opens up, I'll call them."

"...Anything else?"

"...Other than the mayor, no."

Alfano pulled out the drawer to his desk and gathered up the manila envelope he used to hold the evidence for his investigation. Each bombing added to his envelope and to the number of dead. He added more pins to the map; still no pattern emerged. The bombs had been placed all over the city, no repetition, no common subject or target. The man seemed to be a ghost in a bitchin' car. The car said money, money said elegance, maybe some class, the man wasn't a thug, maybe educated. He was methodical, he had specific tastes and habits, the cigarettes told him that. He's an older man, patient and precise, sees the goal line and won't be deterred. A loner, Alfano guessed, but amiable, considering the gullible assistants he used then discarded. He was either Irish or English then again maybe not, perhaps Scottish or maybe even Welsh, any one of these was possible. Knows dynamite and explosives, maybe ex-military, age would be right, maybe a miner at one time.

At 9:30 a.m., Alfano climbed into the Packard and headed downtown, he knew this wasn't going to be fun. The mayor may have had some time to cool down, but there had been time for the papers to get involved. He stopped at a newsstand and picked up a copy of the *Tribune*, latest edition. "*Bomber Strikes at Mayor's Heart*" was the headline. The news only got better as he read the article. All the rumors of a war between Kelly and McCormick seemed to be confirmed. There was an almost gleeful tone to the story over the bombing of Ward 11; the word retribution was used twice. There was one sentence about the dead Malloys, no names, and the impact the bombing was having on the community. The only quote, at the bottom of the column, was from His Honor, "We will rebuild the Ward 11 building and we will make it better. The fair will go on."

Why would the mayor mention the fair? That put a strange thought in Alfano's head. *Yes, why mention the fair at all.*

Gini beamed as Alfano walked into the mayor reception area. The lighting was poor, but Alfano managed to see the Laurel and Hardy boys sitting on their usual perches.

"…Detective."

"Miss Gale, I have an appointment with the mayor." Alfano winked.

"He'll be available soon, Commissioner Hayden is with him."

"Wonderful," Alfano said and walked over to the two men. "How are you two lapdogs, has the commissioner thrown you your bone today?"

"What was that remark?" the skinny man asked.

"Bone, tidbit, treat, you know, something you give a dog for being a good boy."

Hardy stood, "What the hell is this roust all about, we work for the city, just like you."

"Hardly, there are no clowns in the police department."

The skinny fellow stood up, their conversation was interrupted as the mayor's office door opened. Commissioner Hayden stuck his head out.

"Play nice, Detective, they are most helpful when the chips are down. The mayor will see you now."

Alfano tipped the bill of his fedora toward the lapdogs and walked into the office, as he passed Gini, he tapped her desktop and smiled.

"...Detective."

"Miss Gale."

Another man stood in the office, his back to Alfano. Alfano knew Patrick Nash; he wasn't the least bit surprised that the man was in the meeting. Since the death of Anton Cermak, the universe of Chicago politics had changed. It was transforming under the all-embracing hold of Nash and Kelly.

"Detective, have you met Mr. Nash?" the mayor asked.

"Good morning, sir, nasty business this is," Alfano said, extending his hand.

"Yes, Detective it is, all the more reason to stop it right away. Let's sit."

Nash pointed to a cluster of comfortable chairs as if it was his office; he was the first one to sit, then Kelly, finally Hayden and Alfano.

Alfano looked at the Irish faces that surrounded him. *So this is the way it's going to be.*

"Detective, may I call you Tony?" Nash said.

Alfano didn't answer.

"Well, Detective, it seems we are getting a lot of calls from the national press, they are concerned about all of these bombings. Some newspapers are suggesting that people avoid Chicago until this all blows over. Well, we can't afford that; we need to start out with a bang."

"...No pun intended, I'm sure," Alfano responded.

"What? Oh yeah, yeah, very funny. But we mean it. This man has to be found and soon. Edward was telling me that you're a good guy. Straight, you even took down some of those guinea bastards during the gang wars."

"Sir, in case you haven't noticed, I'm Italian, on my mother's and my father's side."

Nash looked at him as if he was seeing him for the first time, "Oh, yeah, sorry. Meant nothing by it, but you *were* effective."

"I believe I was. What does that have to do with all this?"

"Well, there's a rumor going around that the fellow might be Irish and that wouldn't be good."

"Mick, Chink, Dago, Spic, I really don't fucking care. My job is to find the bastard and stop him, fair or no fair. He killed a friend of mine and many others; he's a merciless sick fucker. And he may still have one hundred and fifty pounds of dynamite hidden somewhere. That can cause a lot of pain and suffering. His targets are all over the board, but they are all directed at groups, businesses and industrialists, bootleggers, politics and now your party. What's next? I haven't a clue. But I know there will be another one soon and others after that." Alfano stood, walked across the room and headed for a pitcher of water on the far table.

"Jesus, Mary, and Joseph, calm down, Alfano," Hayden offered.

Alfano turned to Hayden, 'fuck you' was written on his face, nothing more need to be said.

"I need to get back to work. If you have something to offer me, let me know. Commissioner, you said you would give me some help, that's great. What are you offering? Do you have any clues, some ideas, any evidence I might need?"

"Well, I can spare some men."

"Wonderful, then I become a personnel manager, not a detective. What I want is to be left alone, don't call me in here for informal political chats. I will pass on information when I have it; you will be the first person I inform about an arrest, but only an arrest. I won't be passing any information to city hall. There are too many loose strings, too many ears and too many things that can spook this guy. That includes the papers, tell them nothing, whatever you do, don't tell them I'm the detective running the case. Now, gentlemen, I have a bomber to catch." Alfano put his hat back on and walked to the door. When he turned the knob, he saw that his hand was shaking. *Fuck them, fuck all of them.*

Gini looked at Alfano as he walked out and shut the door behind him.

"These walls aren't that thick, Tony."

"And I wasn't that quiet either." He smiled and looked at Hayden's men. "They give you any trouble."

"None, quiet and well mannered, like two little lambs."

He leaned across the desk for two reasons, to whisper, "I'll call you tonight," and to take a cheap look down her tight sweater. As if to encourage him, she took a deep breath, a beatific smile painted with red lipstick.

"Later," she mouthed.

He tipped his hat to Gini, turned to the two Hayden men, "See ya, boys," and headed out to LaSalle Street.

# 18

DAVIES ORDERED ROOM SERVICE the next morning and requested that the *Tribune* be delivered with the meal. He was not one to admire his work too closely; he knew that bravado and hubris were a sure way to make a mistake and get caught. He would get to California one way or the other; the best way was with money, Los Angeles, with all its earthly stars in the heavens, was where he was headed. Young women would be eager and willing for his attentions, all he had to do was flash some bills. The newspaper seemed to revel in the destruction of the 11th Ward building. Not in so many words but if you read between the lines, one could find a lot wanting from the article, especially sympathy. The story's tone was a righteous comeuppance for the politics of the city, especially Mayor Kelly. Patrick Nash's name was mentioned in the article twice, for no other reason but to associate him with Kelly. Davies was becoming very impressed with his client; he had thought this all out quite well, quite well indeed.

WLS was on in the background, some morning show that didn't interest him; what he was waiting for was the news, any news of the bombing. Other than the actual facts of the bombing, there was little speculation beyond what the *Tribune* had volunteered. All of which was wrong, as they would soon find out. The latest *Life Magazine* sat on the coffee table, the cover was primarily blue in color, with a bright spring bouquet and a sweet young thing gently brushing flower petals into a dust tray. He paged through the magazine until his eye caught a picture of his pride and joy. *"Ford Model B Coupe - New and Just For You,"* the ad copy captioned. *Yes, just for me, just for me.*

Garon Davies had owned the Coupe for just five weeks; he'd purchased it with some of the original deposit money from his client. He had taken the train to South Bend to buy the car from a dealer recommended by a friend in Denver. He had given them the address of an empty South Bend lot as his current residence. He'd tipped the dealer for all his help and gotten the plates much quicker than usual. *Yes, the wonders of money.* The car was a deep red, a rich red; at night it looked almost black, Ascot Maroon the dealer had said, very classy.

Mrs. Doolittle presented him with a problem, one that needed to be resolved before he left for California. She was cute, in a mid-thirties sort of way, easy on the eyes, the boy a charmer, so well mannered. Under different stars, who knows what the gods might have suggested. But it was not his way, never had been. His goal was simple, to retire to Los Angeles, to live out the few years he had left in the warmth of the west. He was tired of the cold, the cold of his Pennsylvania childhood, the cold of Denver and the Rockies and the cold of Chicago. His skills had been needed everywhere he went, mountains were moved, coal seams ripped open, and, for the right price, villains had been taught a lesson. They were all the same to Garon Davies, rock or people, all needing to be tamed. Mrs. Doolittle and her son would be taken care of, he would see to that.

He strolled down Michigan Avenue to the six-year-old Gothic tower of the Tribune tower that sat directly across the avenue from the Wrigley Building. Davies stopped and gazed upward at the crenelated gargoyle-infested crown. The whisper of a spring breeze coming in from the lake ruffled the flags that stood at attention on the plaza. The little bit of peace that existed was disturbed by the street traffic rattling the iron grating of the bridge that crossed from the north side of the Chicago River to the south. He took the stairs down one level to Hubbard Street. Here, along the river and under the Michigan Avenue tunnels, the dark underside of the city was connected from east to west. A long arcade with windows and doors at the base of the Tribune Tower paralleled Hubbard Street, providing some cover from the hard winters. Walking the length of the arcade toward North St. Clair Street, he heard boxcars slam into each other. The railroad tracks paralleled the river along the north side of the river and passed under Michigan Avenue. A multi-layered world of roads and railroads surrounded him. As he circumnavigated the building, he looked for any place to park a taxi or truck. On the Illinois Street side of the tower, he was pleasantly surprised to see a taxi stand; three hacks were idling near the Illinois Street entry to the tower. He continued west, under Michigan Avenue, to Rush Street, he hailed a taxi and took a ride north on Michigan Avenue and back to the Drake Hotel.

For two days, Davies enjoyed the hospitality of the Drake Hotel, its bar and the small cigar store that carried his PLAYERS. He walked the bright lights of North Michigan Avenue and gazed at its stores; he ate in swell restaurants and enjoyed Carole Lombard's latest movie *Supernatural*. It made him yearn for the Los Angeles and Hollywood scene all the more. The Tribune Building job never left his mind for more than five minutes.

He collected his mail at the central post office, one letter addressed to Mr. Smythe. It was from his client, neatly and professionally typed.

*Dear Mr. Smythe,*

*I want to compliment you on your activities of the last two weeks; they were carried out with professional skill. As I'm sure you have noticed, there are just two items left on the list. I have no doubt they will be executed with your usual thoroughness. All are preludes to the final act, of which you are well aware; it must be accomplished on May 27th.*

*This date must be met to ensure the greatest impact on all concerned. I am not a petty person; I am one of serious rationale and intent. The Bible states specifically that vengeance is the Lord's, in reality, as in this case, He occasionally needs help. You are my sword of vengeance and retribution. Through you, I will be at peace and begin to mend my shattered heart.*

*You have left no witnesses and have been extremely careful, but do understand that the detective assigned to this case is getting closer to assembling a picture of you and your activities. It may become necessary, at some point, to prevent this man from learning more about you, if you understand my meaning. His name is Anthony Alfano and he works out of the South Racine Station, his address is 2183 Ohio Street.*

*At the completion of the final item, you will receive your final payment and we will no longer need each other. When you have completely read and understood this letter, please burn it.*

Davies reread the unsigned letter twice and then lit the corner of the parchment with his lighter. From his room, he watched the sun set across a calm Lake Michigan, the sky was clear, the weather was fine. But the burnt remains of the note portrayed a different story. A storm of fire and avengement would soon be on the heads of the apathetic, indifferent citizens of Chicago.

The next morning, his short holiday over, Garon Davies packed his leather suitcase and called the desk, requesting that a porter take his things to the car. The last stop, after checking out at the front desk, was to buy cigarettes at the cigar shop. A man stood at the counter, displaying something to the cute blond behind the counter, he was of average height, dressed in a dark double-breasted suit, wearing a coal grey fedora with a black satin band. Garon immediately thought he was of Italian descent; the man sported a thin, fashionable mustache.

The girl looked at Davies, "I will be right with you, Mr. Smith." She turned back to the man at the counter, "Well I don't know, Detective, we have a lot of customers who ask for PLAYERS, as you know, thousands of guests come and go here. We try our best to have as large a selection as possible to meet their needs."

"I understand, is it possible that the man might not have been a guest?" Alfano asked.

"I really wouldn't know, we are just a news and tobacco shop, we do not ask for identification. And tobacco is still legal, isn't it?"

"Please, just answer the question, no editorials."

"Certainly, officer, I apologize. We sold some boxes recently; there were two men from London that stayed here, they each bought a couple. There was an Irish gentleman and an Indian. Not the red kind, this gentleman was from Bombay or somewhere. He was very hard to understand. But then again, I'm only the day-girl; the owner of the shop comes in at 6:00. Maybe he knows."

"Have names?"

"Sir, I never ask them for their names. That is highly irregular and against the hotel's policies."

"Do you know who might know?"

"…The front desk, Detective." Alfano turned and headed toward the door.

"I can help you now, Mr. Smith."

Mr. Smythe was gone.

The sales girl paused for a second before she said: "Detective, *that* man occasionally purchases PLAYERS, you might ask him if he knows of anyone else."

Alfano quickly walked back to the counter, "His name, you called him Mr. Smith. Why?"

"Oh, he's a harmless old gent, Irish, I'm sure, sweet. He stops by here often, says he travels a lot and I remind him of his daughter in Denver. Well, I've heard that line before, so I blushed a little. But seriously, he's quite the gentleman; you can tell by the way he dresses, stylish and neat." She caught herself. "Then again, I do talk too much."

"Do you know his whole name?"

"…No, most certainly not. That would be too forward. He told me his name some time ago, don't remember why. So that's what I call him, Mr. Smith."

"I'll take a pack of Luckys and a box of those PLAYERS."

As he stuffed the cigarettes into his coat pocket, he handed the clerk his business card. "If he comes back, can you call me? I would sure like to talk to your Mr. Smith."

Alfano walked quickly through the lobby to the curbside drop off, the valet stood at the top of the step. "Help you, sir?" Seeing the detective, he said, "Sorry, didn't recognize you, sir. Your car, I'll bring it around."

"Did a gentleman in a tweed jacket and dark red bow tie just leave, I meant to give him something and forgot. Damn shame if I miss him."

"Oh, yes sir, Mr. Smith. Nice fellow. Always with a good morning and a hello, reminds me of my grandfather, dapper he is and all. In fact, that's his car at the corner." The valet pointed to a deep red Ford that was turning onto Michigan Avenue, Alfano watched it accelerate north toward Lake Shore Drive.

Alfano knew that by the time he got his car, Mr. Smith would be long gone. He turned back to the lobby.

"Your car sir, would you like it?"

"It's Detective Anthony Alfano, kid and yes, bring it around. I'll be right back."

Alfano spent ten minutes at the front desk, trying to get as much information about Mr. Smith as possible. First, he learned it was Smythe, not the more familiar Smith, secondly, he stayed at the Drake every few months, and the last, he left an address in Denver as his permanent address.

"Are you sure that this is his address?"

The desk clerk looked at Alfano like he'd been asked if he was a Republican. "Detective, we have thousands of guests staying at our fine hotel and I am very sure some of them are not who they say they are as recorded in our guest book. And we do not check on their veracity."

"Cut the bullshit, what room was he in?"

"312."

"Thank you, now kindly hand me the key."

"Don't you need a warrant or something?"

"…Not really, if you give me the key and your permission. But, if you insist, I'll have fifty cops here in ten minutes, they'll fill your lobby and crowd your entrance, their squad cars will block up the street. How would that work for your guests?"

The clerk handed Alfano the key and directed him to the elevator.

Arriving at room 312, he caught the maid just before she was going into the room. "Have you been in there yet?" Alfano asked, holding up his badge.

"No, sir," the thin black woman answered. "I don't want no trouble."

"None to give you, I'll tell you when the room can be cleaned."

Alfano opened the door and took a quick look around, seemed like any normal room after a guest had just left. Unmade bed, the curtain opened to the view of the lake, used glasses, an empty bottle of Jameson whiskey and a full ashtray. He ignored the obvious ashtray and looked through the bathroom, nothing except used soap. "Any personal toiletries would have left with him," Alfano offered to no one, talking to himself. He looked between the sheets, clean, under the bed, nothing. There was nothing in the closet either. "He's neat as well." He examined the glass and was not surprised to find it clean of fingerprints. The glass smelled of whiskey, but there were no prints on it or the bottle. He knew the man was thorough and he was confident that this might be his man. Even when Mr. Smythe thought he was safe, he took precautions. The butts in the ashtray were all PLAYERS, but what intrigued him most was the burnt piece of paper sitting on top of them. He could read nothing on the large black fragments that had been left, obviously a note or something. A *Tribune* sat folded in two on the side table; it was open to page two, the ongoing story of the 11<sup>th</sup> Ward bombing.

"Reading about your handiwork, Smythe?" Alfano picked up the paper and opened it, an envelope slipped out from between the pages and drifted lazily to the carpet. The address said Mr. Smythe, General Delivery, Central Post Office, Chicago, Illinois. It was canceled with today's date stamped on it. From Chicago Central Post office; the date was today. Of course, there was no return address.

# 19

GARON DAVIES took a quick look in the rearview mirror and watched as the man from the cigar shop talked with the valet, the stranger then shot him a direct glance. Not rushing the turn, he slowly increased his speed until he merged with the northbound traffic of Lake Shore Drive. His heart pounded, he felt adrenalin coursing through his veins, he held the steering wheel tight. *Close, too damn close.* He knew he'd messed up, the cigarettes. *Damnation, they will be the death of me yet, intentional or otherwise.*

He continued north to Elmhurst and pulled into a park fronting on Lake Michigan. He lit one of the offenders and blew the smoke out toward the lake. There were two jobs remaining, if there was one thing he had always been proud of, it was the completion of a contract. Two left, sixty thousand dollars, enough to make the Coast and the sun.

An hour later, he drove east, then south, until he arrived at his rented garage. He lifted the door and pulled the car into its usual location on the left side, leaving more than enough room to complete the work ahead.

He hated to do it, but he knew it was coming at some point in the contract; he retrieved the roll of masking tape and newspaper and began to block out the chrome windows and trim on the Coupe. After two hours of careful work, he prepared the black paint and filled the reservoir on the spray gun that was attached to a small compressor. He wore coveralls and a mask as he repainted the car, working quickly and efficiently. It took him three hours to transform a maroon car into a black one. The light was fading through the thin cracks around the high blacked-out windows by the time he finished. Satisfied with his paint job, Davies treated himself to a dinner of beans and small frankfurters. He rounded off with a warm beer. Next, he cleared away the dirt from a lock buried in the dirt floor of the garage, unlocked it and lifted an iron plate that covered his hidey-hole. Nesting comfortably inside were three unopened cases of dynamite, coils of wire, four alarm clocks and a steel tool chest that held his money. High above the hole, resting on a rafter and out of sight, was a small tool chest with thirty dynamite caps, half were electric, the others were flammable.

At the workbench, he assembled the various components, wires, batteries, and clocks. Two would be used for this explosion; the second bomb would be a backup. He no longer wanted or needed an assistant; he knew he had been foolish to use them. When all the preliminary assemblies were finished, he placed them in the hidey-hole, closed and locked the lid and obscured the area with dirt and a broken chair. He turned out the light, locked up the garage and headed toward the "L," three blocks away. Thirty minutes later he was smoking a cigarette across the street from Detective Anthony Alfano's apartment, he didn't stay long. The lights appeared to be out judging by the narrow lobby windows that followed the building's interior stair upward. Nothing was backlit. But he was surprised that Alfano's apartment was only one block over from the smashed and burned remains of Jimmy's bar. He began to understand Alfano's interest in him, it was personal for him, he may have known some of the patrons. *So Alfano wants revenge, always a pleasurable experience if properly exacted.*

Davies continued on for another block, caught a taxi on Halsted and directed the hack back to the "L" station. He over-tipped the driver and walked into the station. Ten minutes later, he was at the neighborhood speakeasy, acquiring more courage.

Alfano placed all the bits and pieces of the evidence he'd collected at the Drake in the desk drawer with the others. He took a Drake Hotel postcard and pinned it to the cork board. He also pinned the cover of the PLAYERS cigarette box near the postcard. He secured the cutout picture of the Ford Model B Coupe, from the open page of the *Life Magazine* that was left on the coffee table, next to the cigarette box. Alfano easily got the license plate number; the valet had noted the Indiana plate number on the tag for the keys for the Ford. He was surprised how quickly the Indiana Department of Motor Vehicles had responded with an address. One call to a cop he knew in South Bend confirmed his suspicion, the address was a fake. Even the Ford salesman, when confronted by two South Bend cops, hadn't a clue about the buyer, other than his name.

He had missed the man by seconds, but he had seen his suspect, healthy, possibly Irish or English. He was also able to confirm the cigarettes. The man was also very well dressed, his black and white shoes were polished, and he had a neat silk bow tie. Luckily, Alfano had caught a quick look at the man's face; he had turned around when the girl said, "I will be right with you, Mr. Smith."

For a brief moment, the gods had allowed Alfano to look into the face of evil. He was proud of his skills of observation and interpretation, they were developed and honed over his twenty-two years on the force. Twenty-two hard, difficult years, the scars proved it. Two holes in his shoulder and one through his thigh attested to luck. His skill, even after being shot, was proven by three awards for valor in the line of duty.

An Italian on a police force made up of more Irishmen than there were in most towns in Ireland had set him apart from the rest. The bad guys in Chicago were from the same stock of European immigrants; Capone and Nitti were balanced out by O'Banion and the Moran. Throw in a few Jews for accounting skills and you had the right combination for a real drama full of double-dealing. Most of the trouble started with the goody-two-shoes and the temperance leagues, add in the Federal government and Prohibition and you had the fixings for the real world study of the great economic theory of supply and demand. People wanted liquor and other people were just as eager to get it to them.

Alfano stared at his cork board and then at his notes. Now he had four columns and there was no doubt that all the bombings were the work of Mr. Smythe. There was no comfort to have a name to put to a face, even if he knew the name was a false one. Two hours later, the Denver police called him back and let him know that the address Mr. Smythe had given the Drake was as false as the South Bend address. No surprise there. He did get find out from the Denver sergeant that there were three bombings left unsolved in Denver, one was a union hall and two were banks. The two bank jobs were most curious, nothing was taken; they were just large explosions that destroyed both buildings. Since no one was killed, one bombing was union-related and the banks lost no money, the police didn't try too hard to follow up. Alfano wrote the names DENVER and SOUTH BEND in block letters on two pieces of paper and stuck them to the side of the board.

"Nice board, you closer to finding this fucker," McDunnah said as he handed Alfano a cup of coffee.

"Closer, maybe, if I had an artist, I could try and describe the man, maybe I would end up with a very good likeness, something I could circulate to the guys on the force. By my count, three, maybe four people met and talked with Mr. Smythe, everyone said the same thing, pleasant, well mannered—a gentlemen. They'd be tough to put on a jury."

"They said the spelling was S M Y T H E?"

"Yes, not the normal Smith we usually see here."

"I'll bet you it's a fake name, but he probably didn't travel far from his roots. Smiths, as we know, frequent hookers more than any other surname. They just like the girls more, I guess."

"Funny."

"But it was everywhere in the old country, every other man seemed to be called Smith. I knew a German kid whose father's last name was Schmidt, but he changed it to Smith when he came to this country. Not uncommon. But this spelling is different, why? It's old, something closer to the Old English; the name is more closely related to the blacksmith origins in England. My guess is that it's the oldest spelling of that name."

"We have some of the same things in Italian but they are based on the Latin roots, every language has it. An ironworker from Italy might have the name *Ferrari*, Italian for ironworker."

"True, but from my experience, a man often takes an alias with roots closer to his family. The man's mother perhaps, she may have been a Smythe. We aren't all that creative, no matter how smart we think we are. I'm going to go out on a limb and say the man is English, maybe Welsh, where traditions are a little deeper."

"Any clues about his real name?"

"I'll guess Welsh, something similar, could be one of a thousand names. But he's a wonder with dynamite, the tool of the miner. Wouldn't be surprised if he worked the pits in Pennsylvania or even here in Illinois, when he was a lad. If he's in his late fifties or early sixties, he would have been thirty at the turn of the century, a lot of mining in Pennsylvania at the time. Then there was the strike in 1902, maybe a hundred thousand men walked off their jobs. A lot of men ended up here. Maybe he was one of them."

Alfano looked back at the board and then wrote COAL MINER on a piece of paper and stuck it to the wall.

McDunnah handed Alfano a piece of paper, "A Miss Gale called from the mayor's office, said that the mayor wanted an update and you should give her a call."

Alfano smiled, "Thanks, Sergeant."

"Good morning, Gini, let's meet for lunch and I'll bring you up to speed." Alfano listened to the response. "How about the counter at Woolworths on State?" He listened. "12:30, great, see you then."

Alfano guessed the pressure of all the press calls to the mayor's office was getting to her; she sounded tired on the phone. Hell, he was tired, but the close encounter with the bomber suddenly invigorated him. Now he had a man to chase, not a ghost. He could catch men; he was very good at that.

# 20

FINDING TWO SEATS side-by-side at the Woolworth lunch counter was tough; they waited for five minutes until a young woman got up. Gini asked the man next to her to move over one seat, he grudgingly obliged. They both ordered coffee and the lunch special, meatloaf, and mashed potatoes.

"I really shouldn't, it'll ruin my figure.".

"Your figure is just fine," Tony offered.

"You're a dear, but seriously, I've been eating and drinking a little too much recently." She placed her hand on his thigh and smiled.

"It's the pressure, this man's been tough to find."

"You've found him?"

"No, not exactly, but I've found out a lot since I ran into him at the Drake."

"I couldn't believe it when you told me over the phone. When I passed on your report to the mayor, he was pleased but still extremely concerned. I guess we all are."

"The man was a ghost, now he's real and real men can and will be caught. I'm just having trouble figuring out why he's doing this. There are so few connections between all the bombings, I can't find a common thread."

Their 'Specials' quickly appeared on the linoleum counter

top. The thick brown gravy covered every square inch of the plate's surface; anything could be hidden under it.

"I'm so hungry even this looks good," Alfano said.

Gini looked at the alleged food on her plate, "If you don't mind, I think I'll pass." She sipped her coffee while she looked at Alfano in the mirror secured to the back wall behind the soda fountain. When he noticed, she smiled weakly.

"Tired, I can see it."

"Yes, and I didn't get much sleep either, I was at the mayor's office late last night, Mr. Nash and Commissioner Hayden came in at 6:00 and I had to get them some dinner. By the time I got home, it was past 11:00. But I'll be fine."

They looked again at each other in the mirror. "Is there anything new to report?"

"We are focusing on an Englishman or maybe a Welshman, someone who might have been a miner and a demolition expert, seems to point to that." The noise level in the joint obscured any eavesdropping. Most of the patrons were not in the mood to dally. Wait, sit, order, eat, dash out was the norm at the Woolworth's counter, anyone not following the regimen was likely to get tapped with a passing elbow. When a casual bump caught Alfano on the shoulder, he glared at the man in the mirror, the man said, "Sorry."

"Everyone's on edge," Alfano said.

"Let's get out of here."

As they walked back up State Street toward City Hall, Gini looked at the Carson Pirie Scott building, "I remember walking up this street with Thaddeus. He'd hold my hand, everything was new and bright. The cars and the buses made him all excited. I miss him so much."

Tony put his arm around her and pulled her close. "Cruel losing a child, there's little that can be said."

"More has been said than was really necessary, all the denials, all the excuses, all the blaming, my heart still aches."

No kiss at the entry to city hall, just a quick hug, Gini went through the doors and Alfano walked slowly back to his car parked in the LaSalle Street garage. *All the denials, all the excuses, all the blaming, her pain is still there, even two years later. Glad I never lost a child; I don't know what I'd do.*

Two more taxis had been reported stolen during the night, one to the south, near 17th Street and Western Avenue, the other, a Checker, on the north side, near Wrigley Field. The 17th Street cab was recovered near 79th and Western; it was chalked up to a joy ride headed south. The Wrigley cab theft had not been solved. The driver had gone into an all-night diner for a quick coffee and a pee. The night had chilled and he'd left the taxi running. When he came out five minutes later, it was gone. Alfano drove up to the Checker offices; he'd called and asked the company to detain the driver until he could get there.

"I'm Detective Alfano, Mr. Hazlett. Tell me what happened."

"Nothing to tell really, been driving for six years now, never had this happen, just got lazy. One screw up and now I'm going to lose my license. These bombings got everyone on edge, especially us cabbies since the word is that a couple of the guys that was killed were hacks. That true?"

"Yes, it is, that's why I'm talking with you. If it was my guy, he only wanted the vehicle, not you, you're damn lucky I guess."

"No shit. Sorry about that, didn't mean to say that, just nervous."

"Understood, anything seem different to you, anyone at the diner that was just not right?"

"Been racking my head, was parked right out front, sitting nice and pretty in the diner's bright lights, maybe ten people inside, was 1:30, a quiet night. Wasn't worried, done it lots of times."

"Until this time."

"Yeah, till this time."

"The people inside, any of them leave while you were there?"

"One guy, a dapper sort, was sitting near the door when I came in; I remember him because I thought he'd be the type to need a cab. When I came out of the can, he was gone, didn't notice my cab missing for another two or three minutes until Mack, the counter guy, asked me what happened to my taxi. I spun around and saw it was gone. All for a piss and a cup of coffee, I'll probably lose my job. Damn it all to hell."

"Mr. Hazlett, I'll see what I can do to help you. Have you ever seen this dapper fellow in the diner or elsewhere?"

"Not that I recall, been going to Mack's for five or six years, first time I ever had any trouble, but my hours are late, for all I know this guy could go there every day at nine and I wouldn't know. I'm sure Mack would know if the guy comes around a lot, he's got a great memory."

Mack did have a great memory; he could only place the guy in his diner once or twice during the past year. Not recently though, he only remembered the man that night because he asked for a pop, not coffee, "Said he didn't want to be kept up all night. We laughed about it and then he was gone, hadn't even touched his soda, it still sat on his table. But he did leave a buck for the effort. Poor Alan, too bad about his cab."

"Alan Hazlett, the cabby?"

"Yeah, he's a good man, two kids, and a sweet wife. Came in here a few times when he was off duty, said they were on their way to a Cubs game, just a few weeks back. Damn shame; hope he doesn't lose his job."

"I'll see what I can do," Alfano answered. "What did this soda pop fellow look like?"

Mack's description fit Mr. Smythe down to the bow tie and the polished shoes. Alfano was sure he was his man. Mack also said he'd walked in; maybe he was from the neighborhood.

"Most of the patrons live in the area, a lot of them have apartments and either can't or won't cook, so I'm sort of their restaurant of choice. Besides I'm reasonable."

"If the man stops by again, can you give me a ring?" Alfano passed him his card. "Don't make a production of it, just say you're calling about the meat order or something if anyone asks."

"Yeah, I get it; if he comes in, I'll call. My guess is I won't be seeing Mr. Suave here again."

"…Mr. Suave?"

"Yeah, I give all my customers a name, especially if I don't know their real one. He is Mr. Suave."

"Got it, thanks, Mack. By the way, what are you going to call me?"

"…Mr. Nosey."

"Works for me, that's my middle name."


Alfano climbed back into the Packard and spent the next hour driving the streets of the north side neighborhood above Division. *Sometimes luck plays a part in catching the bad guys.* The diner was located on North Milwaukee Avenue, a slashing diagonal street on the neat grid of Chicago that continued from Kinzie Street and Desplaines Street on a northwest trajectory until it disappeared into the farmland, somewhere west of Waukegan. For a good bit of its route, it paralleled the "L" into the Loop. Today, the best-dressed people Alfano saw walking the streets were two priests from St. Sylvester's on Palmer Street. But he also noticed the trees were beginning to leaf out, a touch of green on some, more on others. He could tell which part of Italy a man was from by looking at him, but he couldn't tell an oak from an elm. So to him, a tree was a tree and a forest was a forest, but a Neapolitan was a lot different than a Sicilian, which was a good thing to know some days in some alleys.

He drove past the Polk house, a police car sat out front; a cop leaned against the side door, talking to a gang of kids. He stopped, rolled down the window, flashed his badge and waved the cop over. The patrolman, obviously not in a hurry, took his time crossing to the middle of the street.

"Nice car, what can I do for you, Detective?"

"How long you been here?"

"Too long. Usually, they drop me off; today I was able to take a car. Why?"

"Anybody drive by, well dressed, seemed to take an interest in what happened here?"

"I get five lookers an hour; everyone wants to see the house, nobody special, if you know what I mean."

"No, enlighten me."

"Just gawkers and thrill seekers, people that need something else to do, I'm here to discourage those looking for souvenirs. You'd be surprised what people would take if I wasn't here."

"I doubt it, seen too much already, what people will do when no one's looking. Anybody local say anything about the Polks? Things they might not tell a detective or somebody else."

The patrolman looked back at the house and the three boys standing on the sidewalk next to their bikes. He waved at the tallest, "Davey, you want to come over here?"

Alfano noticed that Davey did not want to talk with anyone.

"David, get your ass over here," the cop ordered, taking Alfano by surprise.

"Sometimes these punks need some encouragement." He

turned back to the group. "In fact, all of you get over here."

The gang pushed their bikes over to Alfano.

"Davey, tell the detective what you told me."

"I'm no snitch."

"Good, that's out of the way, now tell him about the night of the explosion."

Davey looked at his friends, one finally said, "Tell him for Christ's sake, Davey, tell him."

"No blasphemy, kid, or I'll whack the back of your head and tell Father Hagen," the cop said.

Davey was on the spot now but since his boys were backing him, he began. "I was out taking a walk the night the alderman's house was bombed."

"Kind of late, way past the curfew," Alfano said.

"The old man was in a mood, drunk, so's I knew it was best if I stayed away for a while, curfew or not. Just before the explosion, I was walking down Artesian near Hirsch and I saw this man leaning against a car, smoking. Every once in a while, he'd flick on his lighter and look at his watch. I stayed back, hidden, just curious. He was standing there like he was waiting for something or someone. There was all the noise from the earlier explosion over at the park, I hadn't gone out yet but heard it through my window. So's I thought I might go out and see what was up. This guy just stood there, smoking. Then the loudest noise I'd ever heard came from a few blocks away and the sky lit up from this here explosion." Davey hooked his thumb over his shoulder. "I turned toward Maplewood and saw the flames and all. When I looked back at the man and the car, he'd already climbed in, three seconds later he was gone. Thought he'd turn at Potomac toward the explosion, but no, he went down to Division then turned and went left. Thought it was strange but didn't make no nevermind to me."

"Car, could you tell the make of car?"

"Yes, couldn't mistake it, looked like a new Ford Coupe,

dark color, best I could do."

"This help any, Detective?" the cop asked.

"Some. Thanks, Davey."

"Don't I gets something for being honest and all?"

"…My gratitude."

"Gee, thanks a heap," Davey and his gang headed up Maplewood toward Hirsch.

"You believe him?"

"Yes, I do. Said a few things that jive with some other evidence. What's your name?"

"…Dooley, from the California precinct."

"Well, Dooley, keep those baby blues peeled. The bomber lives somewhere in this neighborhood, he drives a deep red Ford Coupe, brand new. Maybe Indiana plates. He's killed a lot of people since the first of the month and I don't know what's going to stop him. So if you see a well-dressed someone in that car, call your station or me. Got it?" Alfano handed him his card. "…Day or night."

"Yes sir, got it. Jesus, Mary, and Joseph, he lives somewhere around here?"

"Yes, good chance."

"Damn."

# 21

DAVIES PARKED the Checker cab in the empty half of the rented garage and immediately pulled off the plates. The flashy checker pattern, alternating black and white squares, wrapped the cab from the front grill to the back end. Black running boards and fenders balanced the black cab over the unmistakable yellow of the body. He pulled the rear seat out, leaving the floor with its rubber mat open from the back of the front seat, the upholstered back split by the usual hump of the drive shaft. He then drilled a series of holes through the floor and threaded in eye bolts, three pairs front and back.

Two cigarettes later, he sat two wooden boxes side by side; they were shallower than the seat he'd pulled out. Flipping the removed seat over, he clipped out the springs and other support structures inside the seat itself, leaving enough to support the seat, but roomy enough to fit like a long upholstered lid over the two boxes. The canvas on the seat would disguise the real contents. After fitting the boxes and seat together a few times, he was confident that no one would think there were fifty sticks of dynamite under the passenger seat. If they did, it would probably be their last thought. It was late, he would finish the mechanism tomorrow; he still had three days until the required completion date on the contract.

Opening the side door, he looked up and down the dark street, shed his jacket and tie, slipped them into the paper sack under his arm and grabbed an umbrella near the door. Lighting a PLAYERS, he locked the door behind him and began walking the few blocks to his apartment. A misty rain had started, giving the streetlights a softer glow; the umbrella hid him in its shadow. At the front door, he closed and tapped the umbrella softly against the banister, knocking off the rain.

"Is that you, Mr. Smythe?" Mrs. Doolittle said through the open crack in the front window.

"You are up late, Mrs. Doolittle."

"Couldn't sleep, head's all in a muddle. How was your trip?"

By this time Davies entered the building and walked to the foot of the stairs, Mrs. Doolittle was standing in the open door. "It went exceptionally well, accomplished everything I set out to do. The timing was perfect, the orders were sent and I have a few days to enjoy the spring. How's Ralph?"

"Doing well, went back to school yesterday. He tells me he was the envy of the kids, his story of the hospital and all."

"I wouldn't be surprised. He's a good kid, you should be proud."

"I am but he still misses his father and it's all I can do to provide for him. But we'll get by, thank you very much. I don't want no handouts; they always seem to come with strings."

"Know exactly what you mean, I've been down that road a few times with the unions many years ago. Those days, you didn't know who to trust."

"I never figured you for a union man."

"You had to join it to work, my father would say, 'Sometimes you have to dance with the devil to put food on the table.' We never starved, but there were days my stomach ached. Not now though, life has been good for old James Smythe, real good. You have a good night, Mrs. Doolittle, please get some sleep. I'll be here if there's trouble."

"Do you expect trouble?"

"No, Mrs. Doolittle, I don't, but it's always a good idea to keep an eye open if you know what I mean?"

"I think I do, thank you for being here. Yes, I'll sleep well and you too, Mr. Smythe, you too." She closed the door.

Davies climbed the stairway to his room, secured the locks on the door and made sure the heavy drapes were closed. By the time he fell asleep, the sun was breaking through the thin blanket of clouds left over from the rainstorm. He slept until noon.

With Mrs. Doolittle at work and the boy at school, the house was quiet, perfect for his work, rebuilding the alarm clock. It was much more comfortable than working in the garage. The work was meticulous and required concentration. After two hours, he was pleased. *The best I have ever made and it will be safe until I throw the small switch. Not bad if I say so myself.*

The device wasn't very scientific, a clock to measure the minutes and seconds, a small spring in the clock, released at the proper second, instantly threw another lever onto a metal plate. The lever would be positive and the plate negative, completing the circuit, allowing a jolt of electricity from a battery attached to the device to instantly heat the thin filament of wire nestled within the blasting cap, that heat would ignite the explosive in the shaft of the cap. The small explosion of the blasting cap would trigger the dynamite into which it had been inserted. That explosion, a thousand times more powerful than the blasting cap, would detonate the other sticks of dynamite secured to the first. The subsequent reaction of the fifty exploding sticks would be significantly multiplied. With fifty sticks of dynamite exploding, it would be incorrect to assume it would be fifty times larger than the first stick, the explosion would be much more devastating. Anyone within a block of the explosion would not survive. If the device were properly placed near the supporting structures of a building, it could very possibly demolish the supports, causing the building to collapse. If Davies had adequate time, he would try to do just that, but time was always a problem when placing bombs. There seems to be so little time when trying to be so precise. The yellow Plymouth taxi would have to do; the closer he could park it next to the structural supports of the building on Illinois Street, the better. If he could drive it through the double doors and into the ground floor lobby, that would be ideal, but he did that he would never make it to California.

After a quick breakfast of scrambled eggs cooked over the hot plate and some very black coffee, Davies dressed and headed down the stairs. The Doolittle apartment was empty. He walked the few blocks back to his garage. He had spent two weeks, after he'd received the contract, looking at garages in the neighborhood, trying to find the one with the least visibility. Most of the small homes in the neighborhood were one and two story structures, there were no windows facing the alley and the garage. The garage doors were solid and almost impenetrable, a little of his handiwork strengthened them. He knew that he was tempting time and fate, there were desperate teenagers and young men about, willing to break a door to find something to steal and sell. Every day, he walked to the garage, knowing that someday the door would be busted open or jimmied. Today was not that day as he backed his Ford Coupe out of the garage and into the alley. He drove into the Loop and passed the Illinois Street entry to the Tribune Building and its iconic tower two times. By his third pass, he had picked the locations and the best time. The schedule and the contract would be met.

Davies parked at the curb, opposite the cabstand at the base of Tribune Tower. He smoked a cigarette and went over everything in his head. *One, Alfano has probably discovered that the car was not purchased locally and he knows its color; I have taken care of that. Two, he probably knows that the dynamite was stolen, probably from a nearby quarry, but the baby-girls are well hidden. Three, by now he realizes that the targets are all over the map, none point to any one direction. It is impossible for Alfano to anticipate the next target and the ultimate objective. I am safe for now.*

Then he drove past the small apartment building on Ohio Street. The information was quite clear. The detective was a problem; he would have to be dealt with. He knew that Alfano was getting closer. He knew what Alfano looked like, he was sure that the detective had only gotten a fleeting glimpse of his face, if that. But Davies realized that he didn't have the resources, such as they were, of the Chicago Police Department.

# 22

ALFANO CRUSHED another Lucky Strike butt in the glass ashtray on his desk. It said 'Miami Beach' on its side; it was the only memento he'd acquired from the last vacation he'd taken. *Maybe vacation is not the right term.* He had forgotten exactly when. He vaguely remembered it had to do with a suspension and the death of three gangsters and a shoot-out somewhere on the city's border with Cicero. Later, the police commissioner told him the suspension was all a mistake and that he would take care of it. And it *was* taken care of. Alfano was made the fall guy; he'd lost two months' pay, taken the train to Miami Beach, and was drunk for two weeks. When he returned to Chicago, he had a new ashtray and his badge. He also felt much better when he heard the police commissioner had been caught in a raid at one of Capone's brothels. The commissioner suddenly disappeared, and there were rumors that *he* never made it to Miami. Commissioner Hayden was selected as his replacement.

The cork board was now covered with notes, pictures and newspaper articles. It brooded over him like his maternal grandmother used to, watching his every move, knowing his every thought. His first notebook turned into two and only ten pages were left in the second book. Alfano looked from picture to picture and note-to-note, each was a clue, part of the puzzle, but they needed to see the whole picture.

Sergeant McDunnah sat another cup of hot coffee on Alfano's desk.

"…Answers?"

"More questions than answers."

"That's good, questions are good. Ask me one."

Alfano took a sip, "Why does your coffee taste like shit?"

"Not my coffee, department buys it. I never drink the stuff. Ask another."

"You should be forced to, like a penance. We have this guy, let's call him Mr. Suave, he is methodical, cunning, and seemingly without remorse. He creates, then places bombs made with dynamite; they are getting stronger and more deadly. The bombings happen only at night and he leaves no witnesses. He is a loner, yet he dresses well and has a pleasant personality, according to those that have met him. Friendly was how the girl at the Drake described him, tipped well according to the valet. He likes style and wants to show off, I get that impression from his car. And he has expensive habits, the car and the uptown hotel. However, everything points to an experienced workingman, ex-miner and demolitions expert and, based on his age, someone who may have fought in the war.

"What's this note, says *Wota Klada*?"

"Something new, they took a look at the bullets they found in a Mr. Wota Klada; he'd been found in an alley a few weeks back just after the May Day bombs; he'd been dead for a few days. Mr. Klada was an anarchist and a Bolshevik and he was very close to out dearly departed Mayor Cermak. I rousted him a few years back, he'd been involved with some small-time bombings and thuggery, or at least that was what I saw. But on the q.t., he was given a pass by Cermak and he left town. I heard he went to New York, but nothing more until he ended up back here, rotting in that alley."

"What's with the bullets?"

"They match the same bullet found in Eddy Doyle."

"No shit. So you think this Klada fella was associated with our bomber?"

"Possibly, or at least until he wasn't needed anymore. He was dispensed with just like Doyle and O'Toole and the two Malloys at Ward 11. This man is brutal and sadistic, yet he carries himself like a proper English gentleman. My guess is he's also a charmer and pretends, a facade."

"...A facade?"

"A forged identity, an alias to be sure, maybe has a normal job, one that he tells people about, gives him cover and credibility. Hell, these days, no one dares to ask about your job. If you have a job, then good for you. No questions. A man can hide that way for a long time. I also think someone is paying him, just a sense I have from all that's going on. He's doing this for money and then he'll be gone. I think he's done this before, that's why I have the Denver tag on the board. We have contract killers in the mobs and even a few bombers that do an odd independent job or two. I think that's where Mr. Suave fits in; he's a sociopath and a hired bomber. Not good."

"I would also suggest that whoever hired him is a sociopath and is using Mr. Suave for their own ends. He's getting even for something. That's also something we should also be looking into, Detective. If our man is in it for the money, someone else is willing to spend a lot of money to get even for something. Maybe we should be connecting some of the dots, looking for the promoter. Find him, then maybe we can find the bomber."

"Excellent thought, Sarg, and who do think that person might be?"

"I haven't a fucking clue."

Alfano answered the phone on the third ring, "Good morning, Gini ... The Mayor, what does he want to know?...

Here's the latest," then Alfano suddenly stopped mid-sentence. "Tell his honor that I'll update him later. Working on something, just tell him I'm closer. OK? …Dinner? Can't, wouldn't be good company. Maybe tomorrow … you too, later." City Hall wanted regular updates. All he could think of now was to throw a net over the whole case and say nothing until he had a name, a real honest-to-God name.

The *Tribune's* front page was screaming about the lack of progress finding the bomber. In a column under the newspaper owner's byline, it posed the question on every Chicagoans lips: *"Is this just another cover up by City Hall? It's been almost three weeks and more than two dozen dead and still no bomber in jail? What does City Hall not want us to know?"*

# 23

DAVIES SAID, "I'm going to get a cup of coffee," to the two drivers standing next to their cabs in the taxi zone at the base of the Tribune Tower on Illinois Street. He looked up the height of the building, all lit up with lights, the top was lost in darkness. His Checker Cab sat fifth in line.

"You didn't leave it running?" one of the drivers asked.

"…With all the recent thefts, not a chance. She's locked up tight as a drum, be back in five. Can I get you, fellas, anything?"

"No, I'm good. If I drink any more coffee, I'll pee for a week."

"Nothing for me, thanks," the second hack said as he lit a cigarette.

Davies quick-timed it across Illinois Street to a coffee shop on the corner at St. Clair. He walked the length of the shop to the restroom in the rear. He bypassed the bathroom door and exited into the alley. Three minutes later, he'd already crossed Ohio Street and climbed the short stairs to the parking garage he'd parked his Coupe in earlier. He paid the attendant at the gate and headed west. As Davies crossed Rush Street, he looked at his watch, just one minute more. At Wabash, he turned left toward the Chicago River. At precisely 11:25 p.m., he stopped in the middle of the Wabash Street Bridge, as if his car had stalled. He placed the revolver on the seat, exited the Coupe, pulled open its hood then turned, toward the Wrigley Building and Tribune Tower complex and looked at his watch again. Five, four, three, two, before he could say one to himself, a thunderous roar echoed through the man-made canyons on the opposite side of the river. Smoke exploded in between the towers, illuminated by the bright lights that McCormick had installed to show Chicago the power of the press and the ego-driven magnificence of his buildings. The lights were now obscured by the dirty haze of the shattered Illinois Street façade of McCormick's pride and joy. The few night owls walking the riverfront stood in shock as the dust cloud pushed its way through the buildings and out into the river, toward Lake Michigan. Surprisingly, the city was silent, as if it didn't know how to answer the obscenity that screamed into the night. Davies slammed the hood and climbed back into his Ford. He never noticed the slip of paper drifting out of the car door or the police prowler racing toward him from the south side of the river, its lights were flashing. As he restarted the Ford, the police car slammed to a stop and its occupant, a police captain, put his hand up, signaling Davies to wait.

"What's up, some kind of explosion over there near the Wrigley Building?" Davies asked. "Was that what it was?"

"Why did you stop on the bridge?" the cop asked as he got out of his car. "I saw you, you acted like you were waiting for something."

"Waiting for the carburetor to clear, I guess I flooded the engine; it's new, just getting used to it."

The captain looked back toward the explosion, the dust was settling, but now the clangs and roars of the sirens replaced the echoes of the bomb.

"Let's see some identification, fella. We're on the look-out for coupes like this."

Police cars and fire trucks raced across the Michigan Avenue Bridge toward the Tribune Building.

"...Really, why?" Davies asked as he gripped his revolver.

"Seems this kind of car was used by someone who's doing these bombings, so I'll ask you again, hand me your identification."

"What color is the car you are looking for?"

"Why do you ask?"

"Well, as you can see, this Coupe is black, the one you are looking for is Ascot Maroon, am I right?"

"What? How the hell did you know that?" The captain reached for his sidearm. Davies was quicker and put a bullet into the officer's forehead. Before the dead man hit the metal grating of the bridge, Davies was back in the car and accelerating. He turned right on Wacker Drive and followed the curve until the Washington Street Bridge then he headed west until he was twenty blocks out of the Loop. When he reached Western Avenue, he turned north. Twenty minutes later, he pulled the Ford into the garage, locked the doors and walked back to the apartment. Mrs. Doolittle was asleep in the chair in the front room; the radio was playing a haunting clarinet tune that escaped out the open front window. Throwing the revolver onto the bed, he poured himself a Jameson and shot it back quickly, "Courage, me boy, courage."

Now dressed in dark clothes, Davies quietly walked back down the stairs and out to the street. Mrs. Doolittle had gone to bed, the front room was dark. The walk back to the garage invigorated him, so did the whiskey he'd consumed. He locked the door behind him and after grabbing a flashlight from the workbench cleared away the dirt and opened his hidey-hole. He flashed a light over the boxes of dynamite, satisfied that all was safe. He took out a well-crafted oiled leather case and placed it on the workbench. After he replaced the hidey-hole cover and the dirt, he opened the case and took out the three primary parts of the German rifle. He attached the barrel to the mechanism and secured the stock. The rifle, custom-made from an original Mauser carbine, was the work of an expert weapons man in Colorado; he had emigrated from Germany soon after the Great War. His skills were evident in the beauty and the construction of the rifle.

Davies waited in the coupe, three blocks east of Alfano's apartment, two hours after the Tribune Tower bombing. An hour later, another car approached, its headlights forced Davies to close his eyes momentarily. It passed by and then stopped in front of the Alfano address. Davies watched as the driver sat there for ten long minutes. Then he saw the flash of the streetlight off the car's door trim as Alfano exited. Leaving his headlights off, Davies approached the apartment building slowly. If the lights were on in the lobby, he would have fifteen seconds to target Alfano through the glass wall of the lobby. When he slowed to a stop, he was even more pleased to see that Alfano was talking with someone at the first landing.


The carnage was intense. Alfano parked on North Michigan Avenue and took the stairs down to Illinois. Like the other bombings, by this time the street was entangled in hoses and fire trucks, five streams of water were directed at the crushed and devastated Illinois Street facade of the tower. Pieces of stone hung on thin strips of metal for a few seconds before detaching from the building and crashing to the pavement. The ground was iridescent as the lights reflected off the shattered window glass. The fire continued to erupt from the fifth and sixth-floor windows. The street was littered with the remains of the taxis and cars that were caught in the explosion.

"How many?" Alfano asked the fire chief.

"Don't know about inside yet, my guys are working their way up now, we've found five on the street, all were drivers for the cabs waiting at the stand. Some people driving by were lucky, just cuts from shattered windshields. Lots of damage to the buildings on the opposite side of the street too, but no fires. Five more injured in the coffee shop on the corner. One of the guys was a cabby who'd just gone in to take a pee, you need to talk with him." The chief pointed to a man sitting on the curb next to a patrolman.

"You okay, buddy?" Alfano asked the cabby.

"…Just finished saying my rosary. You a cop?"

"Detective Alfano, the chief says you might have something for me? What's your name?"

"Laurie, Sean Laurie. Drive for Acme Cabs. Yeah, maybe."

"Why maybe?"

"Well, strange thing. I don't know if he was the one, but I was standing over there talking with this other driver when this bright new yellow Checker comes rolling in and parks at the end of the cue. Nice fellow, he said he was going to get coffee, even asked us if we wanted something, went in the shop there. I'd already had too much so I went to take a leak. Didn't see the fellow anywhere inside, the restroom was empty, I did my business. Strange, I thought, and then, as a walked back to the counter, the whole wall of glass exploded and it went black instantly. Thought I was dead. I heard lots of screaming and yelling. Found my way out here, thought I'd been sent to hell, fire and smoke everywhere. Me and few people helped some of the injured until the firemen arrived. They're over there." Laurie pointed to the sidewalk across St. Clair. Alfano saw about twenty people sitting and lying on the concrete, five bodies were covered with blankets.

"Why do you think it was this cabby?"

"Well, I looked around and saw my cab, it's over there, smashed in and burned so I counted the others that were parked behind me. But the new Checker was gone, just mangled car parts left lying around, like the one over there." He pointed to a door panel against the wall of the building. Its bright door still sported the black and white checker pattern band and the name Checker. "If I ever find that son of a bitch, I'll cut his heart out and make him eat it."

Alfano looked at his watch, midnight, forty-five minutes since the blast. Three cars turned down St. Clair and headed directly for him.

"Shit," was all that Alfano could mutter as he watched the Mayor and Hayden, along with two other aldermen, exit the cars. They headed toward him; all they were missing was a rope for the lynching.

"I want you off this case, Detective, you are done, through," the Mayor said. "That's five bombings and this is the worst. McCormick has already called me; he'll be here in twenty minutes, he was at home."

Surprisingly, Hayden came to his defense. "Let's not be hasty, Mayor, Alfano's doing his best."

The Mayor shot Hayden a look, "If this is the best he can do, the whole city is in fucking trouble. What do you know, Alfano?"

Alfano told him everything he knew up to the point of the Tribune explosion. Halfway through the exchange, a sergeant walked up to the group and whispered into the commissioner's ear. All Alfano saw was shock on Hayden's face. Then he watched as he passed on whatever information it was to the Mayor.

"God damn it," the Mayor yelled. "What was his name?" The mayor turned to the sergeant.

"Captain Frank Kennedy, he was found dead in the middle of the Wabash Street Bridge. He was next to his car, shot in the face."

"He was your captain, Alfano, from your damn precinct, wasn't he?" Hayden said.

Alfano rocked back on his heels as if he'd been slapped

with a blackjack. "Where did you say?"

"Wabash Street Bridge, a taxi driver found him and called it in, happened just after the explosion."

"Did the cabby offer anything else?"

"Said that a black Ford Coupe passed him on Wacker as he waited on State, the guy was in a hurry. No other cars about, was about 11:30, he turned right on Wacker and saw the cruiser sitting on the bridge. A body lay next to it. He called it in, but the man was dead. One of the patrolmen knew the Captain; they went to the same church."

Alfano walked away from the group… *a black coupe? If it was the bomber, he's either changed cars or painted it. The bridge would have been a good place to watch from a safe distance, views north or east. But if he's true to his habits, he'll be back in the near north side neighborhood where he's been seen before.* He turned and started toward the stairs that lead to Michigan Avenue, one level above Illinois Street.

"Where the hell do you think you're going, Detective?" the Mayor yelled.

"…To find a killer."


He slowed as he passed Gini Gale's apartment, trying to make up an excuse to stop, but then he continued west. He knew it was a fool's errand, thinking he could find this killer by driving around the streets of the Near North Side. But he'd had enough of the Mayor and the Commissioner; he'd like nothing better than to throw it all back in their laps. But he'd never quit anything and he sure wasn't going to start now.

After two hours, crisscrossing the grid of dark streets, he pulled to a stop in front of his apartment and sat there, going over everything that had happened the past three hours. It was 3:00 a.m. The killer must have a garage, it was all he could think of, there was no new Ford Coupe, black or maroon, parked on any street in the area. A garage was the only answer. But every alley had at least thirty garages flanking the passageway; there were thousands of garages across the northern neighborhoods. *That's more than anybody can search.* Alfano climbed the stair, not caring if Mrs. Kowalski was standing on her landing. Just then, his luck ran out.

"There you are, why haven't you caught this son of a bitch? WGN says the announcers at the station were nearly killed when the bomb exploded at the building. They are calling for the head of the Mayor and the police chief."

"…They?" Alfano asked, not connecting the two.

"The *Tribune*, the people who own WGN, that's who. Thought you would have known that."

"I knew that, it's all newspaper hype. Go back to bed." He finally looked at Kowalski; he was shocked; all she wore was a thin robe with nothing else underneath. "Jesus, Alice, go back to bed. Please, I don't need all this."

"What? You don't like what you see? You don't like a real woman, Detective?"

"Please, go inside, someone will see you, there's nothing but glass between us and the street. Please."

In a split second, the glass panel above the door exploded, showering the lobby entry with glass. Alfano turned toward Alice Kowalski. She stood there staring at him with a shocked expression on her face as a rosy pattern began to grow above her right breast; she placed her hand over the wound and looked at the blood. A second later, she collapsed to the oak floor of the landing. A second shot embedded itself in the plaster wall just above Alfano's left ear. Before he could react, another bullet ripped off the top of the banister, throwing oak shards across the narrow landing. A six-inch piece of hardwood caught Alfano in the right cheek. He turned, bolted up the stair and headed toward his apartment; the stair provided some cover from the glass entry. He called the police and told them he needed an ambulance. Then he grabbed some towels and ran back to Kowalski. She was sprawled across the landing, most unladylike, as blood poured from her shoulder. He rolled her onto her side; there was another hole on the opposite side. *Good, as far as that goes.* He pushed towels behind her and then, using the towels, he put pressure against the wound on her chest. No more bullets interrupted his work as he waited. Ten minutes later, an ambulance arrived and took Mrs. Kowalski to St. Elizabeth Hospital; she was alive, but barely.

The landing was a bloody mess; at least four bullet holes in the walls and stair attested to a marksman needing target practice. Alfano was grateful for this small favor as he took his penknife and extracted one of the bullets. From its weight and size, it was a least a forty-five or maybe even a rifle bullet. He noticed that a couple of the holes went through the Kowalski apartment and out the back of the building. The one slug he found had probably hit the banister. The banister sliver in his cheek had left a small, but noticeable, hole; thankfully it was his only wound, he covered it with a Band-Aid.

For Alfano, now it was personal, the killer knew where he lived.

# 24

THE NEXT MORNING Alfano sat brooding at St. Elizabeth's Hospital waiting for an update on Alice Kowalski. He was at the apartment when Mr. Kowalski returned from his job at the steel plant. Then he drove the distraught man the six blocks to the hospital, the whole time trying to explain what had happened. Kowalski was a basket case. For all of Alice Kowalski's airs and come-ons, Harold Kowalski was the salt of the earth; he loved Alice a lot more than Alice loved him. The good news was that the bullet did little damage other than putting a hole through Mrs. Kowalski's upper shoulder, luckily the bullet missed her lung and every other important organ in that part of her body. Alfano left the Kowalski's and drove to the Racine Station and his cork board stuck with pins and bits of papers.

"What the hell happened last night?" McDunnah said when Alfano entered the station. "The captain is dead, you got shot at and the Tribunc Building was blown up? Jesus, Mary, and Joseph is this man that good?"

"Good and lucky, he was good for most of the night; me, I'm the lucky one. Is your guy available to look at this shell casing and this chunk of lead?"

"Anytime, what is it?"

"I found the casing this morning on the street, probably ejected out the window of his car, the bullet I dug out of the wall. After the last round was fired, I heard wheels squealing, I was too busy with Mrs. Kowalski to look at who was doing the shooting."

"She going to be alright?"

"Yes, and lucky too, three inches lower and it would have been her lung, higher, would have busted out her shoulder. What's the latest about the captain?"

"He left here about 11:15 and headed north to his home, he lives up near Montrose and Ashland. Sometime around when the bomb at the Tribune Building went off, he met someone on the Wabash Street Bridge. There, someone put a bullet in the captain's forehead; he was dead before he hit the street. The captain's pistol never left his shoulder holster. The cabby that found the captain described our vehicle to a tee, but it was black, not maroon."

Alfano looked up from his desk. Gini was standing just outside by the railing that separated the sergeant's desk and the squad room. She rushed to his office and threw her arms around him when he was close enough.

"Why didn't you call me when you got home last night? I had to hear about it through the city hall grapevine. Damn it, Tony, I've been worried sick about you. You could have called."

"I just got in myself, it's been a long night and I'm sorry I didn't call. How did you get here?"

"Cab. But I'm serious, why didn't you call?"

"As you can see, I'm fine, no holes. I did get a sliver in my cheek." He pointed to his Band-Aid.

She stood up on her toes and kissed his wounded cheek, then took one step back and slapped him on his other cheek. "I giveth and taketh away, the kiss was a promise and the other was a reminder to always think of me. Got it?"

"Yes ma'am, I got it."

"I'm doing double-duty, the mayor sent me here to find out what's going on and who shot at you. He thinks I know you from somewhere and can get answers that you won't give him. That true?"

"Which part, the knowing or the getting?"

"Don't be an ass. I think he's concerned."

"Sure he is, McCormick will point this bombing directly at him and city hall. And from my point of view, a lot of the clues do finger City Hall or at least the Alderman Polk and Ward 11 Headquarters bombings. But even the May Day bombings have some connections to downtown, through utilities, trucking, and commerce. Loose connections, I know, but it's still a sticky situation. The bar is another matter, not sure about that, a big question mark over it. And using taxis for each of the bombings makes me think the man has it in for the cab companies. If anything, it makes you think twice about hailing a cab. I got a report yesterday that the cab companies have seen a drop in their business over the last three weeks. Makes the tourists a little edgy, thinking they might be sitting on a bomb, I guess."

"That's silly."

"Of course, but there you are. So you can report back to the mayor that I'm well, no holes, if he still wants me off the job, fine with me. The guy may not be a good shot, but I hate to think I have to check under the house every night for a bomb or two."

"That's not funny."

The sergeant walked over from his desk.

"Sergeant McDunnah, this is Gini Gale, she is the mayor's secretary."

"Pleasure to meet you."

"And you too Sergeant, can you keep this man out of trouble?"

"That's easier said than done, Tony thinks it's his sworn duty to stick his nose in places it doesn't belong."

"Sergeant, that's why I'm called a detective."

"Sergeant, just do the best you can, I'm a little fond of this man."

"I will try; I still light a candle for your son at mass."

Taken aback by the remark, she looked at McDunnah, "That's nice, thank you, but why?"

"I was the first cop on the scene after he was struck, broke my heart. I was the one who picked up the puppy and gave it back to you."

Gini looked at the sergeant and stiffened suddenly as everything, every detail, came back to her.

"Are you okay? Let me get you some water."

"Sit," Alfano directed her to a chair. He gave her the water. "Better?"

Gini took a deep breath and let it out slowly, she looked at the sergeant. "Thank you, I remember now, some parts of that day just come and go. Thank you. It was all so hard and Tony helped me get through it. But now, I can get through most of the day, some weeks go by without too much crying. But I will never forget."

"No one wants you to, Tad was a great kid," Alfano offered. "I wish I knew him better."

"I had hoped that you would." Gini looked at her watch, "I need to go. I told the mayor I would be back in a couple of hours."

"Sergeant, have one of the boys drive Mrs. Gale back to city hall."

The sergeant nodded.

"That would be nice, thank you. And it's good to see you again, Detective Alfano, and you too, Sergeant."

"I'll walk you out," While they waited for the patrolman to drive to the front of the building, Gini whispered in his ear.

"Pick me up at 8:00, I could really use a drink."

An hour after Gini left, the sergeant walked back to Alfano's desk. "She's nice, been through a lot, it still has her, though. Losing that kid's been tough and so was the aftermath."

"…Aftermath? I knew things were rough but what are you talking about?"

"A lot was left out of the final reports. Seems that the driver of the sanitation truck was drunk, or at least a little under the influence. She wanted to press charges against the man, but the word came down that it was ruled an accident so nothing happened. There were at least five witnesses that saw the dog run away from the boy, then he ran after it. The driver, sober or drunk, could not have stopped, so it was ruled a tragic accident. Gini pushed for some type of hearing, Mayor Cermak said no. That was two years ago. Her first husband had died before the boy was born."

"I knew that, car accident, T-boned by a taxi."

"Right and then that other fellow showed up right after the boy was killed."

"The German, I thought he lived downstairs?"

"Right, then he took off with what savings she had. She needed money, so Kelly found her a job in city hall working directly with Cermak; she had been working in the secretary pool, under Thompson. When Cermak was assassinated, she became Kelly's secretary. Strange world we live in."

"What do you mean?"

"Well, Edward Kelly was in charge of the sanitation department at the time of the child's death. He found Gini a better job, then he decided that the death was accidental and any charges against the driver should be dropped. So you never know."

Alfano stroked his pencil thin mustache, thinking, "You're right, you never know."

Davies walked to his apartment; the sun cracked through the thick overcast Midwestern sky briefly, throwing long shadows across the sidewalk and the street. He saw the light on in Mrs. Doolittle's front parlor. He was pissed at himself for missing the shot. It was no more than target practice, should have been easy, a piece of cake. But that damn woman moved just as he squeezed the trigger, then Alfano disappeared before he could track him through the broken window. Alfano was still alive and probably now seriously pissed.

"Good morning, Mr. Smythe, I didn't hear you go out."

"Snuck out I did, didn't want to wake the boy. Took a long walk, after the trip down south, it was nice to be able to get a little fresh air, a nice constitutional was in order. Are you well?"

"Good, or as best as I can be."

"Troubled?"

"Who isn't, these days? The radio said that someone blew up the Tribune Building; I couldn't believe it, so upsetting. I'm afraid to let Ralph go to school, I am."

"I'm sure he'll be fine."

"I know you are an educated man, Mr. Smythe, but how can you know? There was even a remark that they might stop the fair from opening. Ralph would be very disappointed."

"That won't happen, you needn't worry about that. There are many reasons, most of them good for the city's businesses, to make sure it opens, and besides, City Hall will make sure of it."

"I hope you're right. Would you care for some breakfast, I have some coffee made and Ralph wants to say hello before he goes off to school."

Davies thought about the offer, "I'd be delighted, a real breakfast would be a treat after the night I had."

"Wonderful, wash up and come down in ten minutes. How

do you like your eggs?"

Davies looked around the sparsely furnished Doolittle kitchen, only a diner calendar hung on the wall, Saturday, May 27$^{th}$ was circled, the word FAIR was penciled next to it. But there was a domestic comfort about the room even with its Spartan-like decorations. The smell of bacon and toast brought him back to a time he barely remembered, days with similar mornings and aromas, his father at the sink, throwing back a cup of coffee before his turn in the pits. His mother, her thick arm wrapped around her man, a baby snug to her hip as he sat at the kitchen table, now a half-century past.

"Breakfast okay?" Mrs. Doolittle asked.

"Capital, tasty. Thank you."

"Ralph, finish getting dressed. Be a good boy. I'll walk you to school. We leave in five minutes, I can't be late."

"Tell you what Mrs. Doolittle, I'll clean up here and do the dishes, the least I can do. You get ready for work. Don't worry about a thing."

"That's a treat, thank you. And this was nice, very nice. I miss having a man around to cook for."

"Well, that fellow there isn't a man yet, but he will be soon."

"Yes, I will be a man soon and then I will help Mother with everything," Ralph said.

"And I know you will; go get ready for school. School's the best thing for a young man, lots to learn, it will help you when you are a grown man."

"Like you, Mr. Smythe?"

"… Yes, like me."

Davies heard them getting ready; Mrs. Doolittle stuck her head around the corner.

"Thank you again, this has been nice. See you this evening?"

"…Most probably. Study hard, Ralph."

"Yes sir," Davies heard as Ralph went down the hallway, seconds later, he heard the door slam.

He finished straightening the kitchen then headed up to his apartment. Even three cups of coffee couldn't keep him awake.

# 25

ANTHONY ALFANO wished he were anywhere but where he was standing twelve hours after the collapse of the north facade of the Tribune Tower office building on Illinois Street. Colonel Robert R. McCormick, the scion of the McCormick's of Chicago, owner and publisher of the *Tribune* and its news and entertainment empire, stood there glaring at him. Chicago politician, war correspondent, war hero, non-interventionist, an all-around pain in the ass of the Democrats, especially Franklin Roosevelt, the Colonel was shaking with intense anger. It was far more than personal for him.

"Detective, don't even try to cover for that asshole of a mayor. He and all the others in that mausoleum and counting house he calls city hall will pay dearly for this. Their actions or lack thereof caused this. Thankfully, only five souls were lost, it could have been far worse. What have you found out so far?"

Alfano was pissed; he hated being the punching bag for the mayor and now for the *Tribune*. "My investigation is not open for discussion. I report to the commissioner and the mayor, not the press, not even you."

"You will tell me everything. It was the lack of progress that resulted in this effrontery. I will know what is happening."

"Mr. McCormick, if you had been more helpful earlier in the investigation, it might not have come to this. I asked for some help, but your editor said it was the mayor's responsibility to find the bomber, not the newspaper's responsibility. So, here we stand. Are you ready to help me with my investigation now?"

McCormick glared down at the Italian. "I put Thompson out of office and I put gangsters and their ilk in jail. Make sure that Kelly understands that when you see him. He's no better than the rest of his lot, but I'll be damned if they're going to stand in the way of the upcoming fair and more honest politics. You tell him that, Detective." He stormed off, shouting at a gaggle of reporters from the *Sun-Times* and a few of the more ethnic papers in the town. They'd fixated on the Tribune's damage like vultures to a kill.

"That was my office up there, Detective Alfano," a voice said behind him. "I'd left just an hour earlier. If I'd stayed to finish my piece, I'd be splattered all over Illinois Street."

Alfano turned and faced a clean-shaven young man in a gray overcoat and gray hat holding a small notebook. "Who are you?"

"Bobby Murdock, we talked a few weeks back. I called you about an article regarding the bombings and tourists."

"Didn't see it, kid."

"It was put on the back burner, other things were going on. The Colonel called for all hands and here I am. No particular orders, just dig, see what comes up, rattle some cages."

"Don't rattle mine, go away."

"Can't and won't, this story can make a reporter's career and help a detective, like yourself."

"How can you help me? You'd just be in the way." Alfano started to walk away.

"I'll stay on the fringes, but with the right story in the paper and the right information, your eyes can become half a million. People love to solve puzzles, if they think they can help with this one, maybe someone saw something or knows someone. You need witnesses and I need readers. So how about it? Can I buy you a cup of coffee?"

"Do you drink anything stronger?"

"…Depends on the time of day."

"Is this the right time?"

"…Couldn't be better."

Five blocks away, in the core of the old neighborhood, Streeterville, Murdock and Alfano slid into a booth and ordered corned beef sandwiches, pickles, and beer.

"A cop that drinks, who would have thought."

"To be honest, I'm not sure I know a cop that doesn't, but I like your idea, put the story out there. See if anyone knows anything. Where do we start?"

"Not sure really, let's start with what the guy looks like."

"I saw him; I know exactly what he looks like."

"You're kidding, you saw him?"

"From three feet away, he is dapper, well-dressed, sported a bow tie, has thick neatly-clipped gray hair, about six feet tall, with polished two-tone Florsheims. He drives a red, almost maroon, Ford Coupe, but it may be black now – repainted it. Lives somewhere on the near north side, between here and Wrigley Field, and he might be English, Irish or Welsh, was possibly a miner or from a mining family and he smokes PLAYERS. He has something against the city, the mayor, politics in general, and now the *Tribune,* after last night."

"Sounds like a sociopath."

"Yeah, that's my take too. But the kicker is, I think he's being paid to do this. There's been no letters from him, no threats, no ransom demands, and no reasons for his actions. It's like the world only exists to be blown up. He needs money to live; his lifestyle seems to eat it up. He's a bit too pricey for your average hoodlum and those that have met him seem to like him. Fascinating, but it makes him even harder to catch, he really doesn't stand out. Could be your grandfather and you wouldn't even know it. We call him 'Mr. Suave'."

"Nice tag, maybe I can work with it. Can I use all that?"

"Sure, why not. How's the promotion for the fair coming along?"

"Real good, in fact, excellent. We have stories posted all over Middle America, specials for New England and even California. Most papers want to print something more interesting than all the Depression doom and gloom stuff they've been printing. The theme is optimistic and it shows the world all the good things that are going on. There's a rumor that Benito Mussolini is sending a squadron of seaplanes with his second-in-command, Italo Balbo. Now, that will be something. And that squat little man from Germany, Herr Hitler, is sending over the Graf Zeppelin sometime this fall."

"Gangsters, dictators and fascists, great—just what Chicago needs."


Davies didn't know what to do, he was plastered all over the front page of the *Tribune*; everything was there except his picture. The paper even put an outline of a head with a question mark in the middle of it at the top of the column. It was a puzzle for the readers to help solve. *"Help the Chicago Police Department put a face to the question mark. Do you know this man? If so, call this phone number, a five thousand dollar reward is offered if found guilty,"* was in large type under the head shot.

He hadn't bargained for this, all this publicity. The client said it would be over by May 27th. But that was five days away. His final payment would be delivered when the contract was completed. Davies hoped it wouldn't come to this– but now it was spread all over the morning edition of the *Tribune*. There was even an editorial by Colonel McCormick about the need for all good citizens to look around, see anything suspicious, give the newspaper a call. He had to smile at that, give the paper a call, not the police. He'd hoped his anonymity would be his best cover, his shield, now he wasn't so sure. He retrieved another envelope from the central post office, a thick bundle of neatly wrapped fifty-dollar bills was enclosed along with a typewritten note.

*Thank you for your services, only one project left to fulfill the contract. I look forward to its completion.*
*Sincerely*

He hid the $10,000 in the hidey-hole, along with the other $50,000. The final payment of $40,000 would be sent on the 28th of May. He intended to be on the *Los Angeles Limited* the next day and on a beach in California three days later. He had five days to prepare for Saturday.

# 26

GINI SAID, "You're sweet, thank you for the flowers," as she placed the spring bouquet in a lavender vase.

"These last few weeks have been nice," Alfano said.

"Yes, they have. Where should I put them?"

Alfano looked around the small apartment, "Why not on the desk?"

"Excellent, why don't you set them there while I mix us a drink? It's been a long day."

Alfano placed the flowers in the far left corner of the desk, moving the typewriter slightly. "They look nice," he said. "When did you get the typewriter?"

"It's on loan from the city, the mayor has me writing some notes and filling in some forms, you know how that is. And besides, you need to work on your vocabulary, that's twice that you said the word nice. Can't you come up with anything more, more precise than just nice."

"It's back to your games, is it? How about enjoyable and beautiful sound any better?" Alfano clacked away at the keyboard; a piece of paper in the roller caught his rambling, *The quick brown fox jumps over the lazy dog. Still remember how it goes, like riding a bike.* "Nice, needs some cleaning, the lower part of the 'g' has some dust in the key."

"Better, trite but better. I've some cleaner around some-where, thanks." She handed him a martini then tipped her glass to his, "To us."

"I like that, to us."

She curled up on the couch and sat the glass on the end table, "Sit here." She patted the couch, "I've missed you."

"Sorry, very little time even for myself since the bombing at the *Tribune*. The articles in the paper have produced hun-dreds of tips and the commissioner gave me three men to help chase them down, so far nothing. The closest thing we got was a couple of ex-cons that were hiding out, spotted by some kids. So maybe some good has come from this."

"Good. But my job is to get you to relax and forget about all this at least for a few hours, is that okay with you, Detec-tive?"

"Hard to forget anything if you keep calling me detective."

"Sorry, just a habit. So, Mr. Alfano, after we finish our drinks, what would you like to do?"

"There's a jazz trio from New York playing at Club Ala-bam, I'll buy you a steak and then we'll see where the night goes."

"I'm ready," Gini answered quickly, "from the top of my head to the tips of my toes," as she wiggled closer.

The Alabam floor show was its usual rowdy fun and the steaks were perfect. When they left the club and walked the five blocks back to Gale's apartment, it started to rain. The streets looked like glass and the lights from the billboards, neon marquees and cars reflected from every damp surface.

"...Cab?" Alfano asked.

"No, a little rain won't hurt, in fact, it feels nice." She tilted here head upwards and stuck her tongue out to catch a drop.

"Sometimes, you act like a child, that's what I like about you."

"Thank you, Mr. Alfano, I will always remember that. You

are too sweet for me."

"And if you stay out here in the rain, you'll melt because you are so sweet."

"Now you're just annoying, cops don't say things like that."

"What do cops say?"

Gini thought for a moment, "Listen, sweetie, this is how's it gonna be. Just me's and you babe, me's and you's."

"I don't even come close to talking like that."

"True, but sometimes a girl wants to be owned, not courted."

The roar of the truck took them both by surprise; Alfano watched a truck roll by, its engine straining with the load. The humpbacked shape was as much an advertisement as the sign on its door, *Chicago Sanitation Department*. The sweet stench of garbage followed in its wake in the thick damp night air. When he turned back to Gail, she stood frozen, stuck, immovable. Her eyes were wide open, unblinking; she just stared at the truck.

"Gini, you okay?"

No answer, Alfano took her hand and squeezed it, nothing, no response, then her hand started to shake. It was as if a switch had been thrown, the truck continued to idle along the Rush Street curb, two black men were grabbing cans, dumping them in the open maw of the back of the truck. With the rain, one man's hand slipped from the handle of an empty can, there was a loud bang on the brick-paved street. The sound hit Gini like a slap.

"What?" was all she could say as she slowly turned to Tony.

"I asked, are you okay?"

"Sure, why wouldn't I be, I'm fine. Let's get out of this rain." Tony hurried to catch up with her as she started to run toward her apartment, away from the sanitation truck.

He caught up with her at the corner at Chestnut. "Stop Gini, stop, what's the matter?"

She was breathing hard, each breath was a gasp; she put one arm on a sign pole for support.

"I had to get away, to run. Couldn't stay."

"Was it the truck?"

"What truck? All of a sudden I was standing there shaking with fear, don't know why, but I had to get away."

He watched the truck move further north up Rush Street, now lost in the clutter of cars and patrons leaving the bars.

"Let me walk you home, okay."

She looked at Tony, her face was wet. He wasn't sure if it was from tears or the rain. He left her at her apartment door, gave her a hug and a goodnight kiss. She apologized for her behavior.

"I wouldn't be much fun tonight, Tony, sorry. But all of a sudden, I'm exhausted, this girl needs her sleep, and besides, this is a big week for the city. The fair opens next Saturday, everyone will be there; I have planning to do for the mayor with the dignitaries coming in from all over the country. Not sure how much time I'll have for you with all that's going on and I know you will be very busy. So, I'm off to bed, sadly, alone, and you have to go find the bomber. Goodnight." With that, she kissed his cheek and closed the heavy glass door behind her.

Alfano stood there watching Gini walk through the lobby toward the small elevator. She never looked back once, when she disappeared, he turned and walked back to the Packard. It started to rain harder.

# 27

DAVIES SAT in the Ford Coupe watching the contractor's trucks enter and leave The Century of Progress World's Fair at the Cermak Street entry. The same type of panel truck entered and left the fairgrounds three times, a different driver and truck each time. Across the side panel of the black truck, '*Otto Spellbinder*' was posted in large letters, underneath it, '*Painting and Finishing, see our work at the Century of Progress World's Fair.*' Davies liked the confident manner of the owner; all the trucks were new, probably recent contracts for the fair. With his small camera, Davies took several pictures of the trucks, he had them processed at a small camera store on Milwaukee Avenue.

The fair would open in three days. It was advertised in the *Tribune* as the most exciting opening of any event in world history. The article touted a technological marvel, the light from Arcturus, a star, would be used to activate the opening night's midway lights by way of a switch at an astronomical observatory hundreds of miles away. The lights would allow the fair to stay open late at night, offering its technological wonders and exhibits to tens of thousands of visitors.

Davies watched, noting the make and model as another truck left the grounds, this one was a cabinetmaker's truck, it was the same model as the Spellbinder trucks, but it was a dark blue. He followed the blue truck to a small building on Chicago's west side, another truck, older, with the same banner, was already parked in the open parking lot next to the building. The driver went inside.

That evening, Davies took the "L" west to within three blocks of the cabinetmaker's shop, walked to the alley, jimmied the lock on the truck's door, and, with a few twists of wires, left with the truck. Fifteen minutes later, it was safely parked in his garage. Within hours, he transformed the blue panel van into a duplicate, including the side advertisement, of one of the Spellbinder paint company's fleet of black trucks.

His patience and observations paid off, the painter's vans typically arrived by 7:00 in the morning. With only a few days left until the fair's opening, he'd noticed that they were staying much later. Two days before the opening, he dressed in painter's clothes and drove the repainted truck to the North Entrance near the Shedd Aquarium. No one stopped him or any of the other trucks from entering; everyone was behind schedule, every minute counted. He parked the truck in an area filled with other contractor's trucks near the administration building, directly across the promenade from the Sears and Roebuck Building. Then he walked the fair grounds. There were guards and official personnel everywhere, but no one stopped and asked the elderly painter where he was headed. Within an hour, he knew exactly what needed to be done and where to do it.

He was impressed by the fair's magnitude and architecture. Great halls could be easily seen with marquees high above the arcades: *Chrysler and General Motors, Hall of Science, Hall of Religion, Egypt* and even an exhibit that said *Hollywood*. All were aligned along the central pedestrian spine that ran parallel to Lake Michigan. Capping the exhibition were two great towers over 600 feet tall that carried the interconnecting *Sky Ride* of spaceship-shaped cars. It was the west tower that interested Garon Davies. It sat nestled behind the southern end of Soldier Field Stadium, a maintenance yard and parking area sat at the tower's base easily accessed by a street that paralleled the Illinois Central Railroad tracks just inside the fairground.

He walked back toward the administration building, casually smoking, committing the layout to memory. Every step would have to be meticulously planned; his greatest fear was that the ride might be occupied and in use before he could detonate most of the remaining dynamite. Unlike the other victims of his handy work, victims that were specifically targeted, he had no animosity for the people visiting the fair and the contract stipulated that injuries be avoided. But there was another stipulation in the contract prior to receiving the last payment, that a second device be placed at the location of the opening ceremonies. As Davies walked past the stadium, he could not help but notice the openings that led to the field, he walked in and casually walked up to a young man holding a clipboard.

"Sonny, what's all this here for?" Davies said pointing to the stage.

"That is where the ribbon cutting will occur, right after the parade. When that's done, the stage will be knocked down, making the stadium sports- ready once again. You with one of the painting contractors?"

"Yes siree, can't wait for this here fair to open. Was here back during the big Exposition in the last century, she was quite a wonder, but that was before your time."

"Yes, all that was five years before I was even born. But my mother had lots of pictures and postcards from that fair. Got me all interested and excited, so I joined the company that's in charge of managing all this. That was five years ago, I can hardly believe that it's opening the day after tomorrow, seemed like it would never come and now here it is."

"I know how you feel, you set your heart on something, thinking it will never come and then boom, it's there."

"Yes, boom, there it is."

"Say, kid, I have some time on Saturday morning, do need some help around here?"

"Boy, could I! Seems everyone's busy with their exhibits and I'm on the short end, so yes, if your boss can spare you, I could sure use some help."

"Laddie, I'm my own boss, working to help out a friend, but I'm on my own. Say, do you know when this is going to open? Some star in the heavens that will start the festivities, quite a wonder if that's the case."

"That's what they tell me, the light from that star started coming here during the last Exposition and only now it's reached Earth, so they will signal when that light reaches the fair."

"Wow, that's amazing. The missus wouldn't understand a note of what you just said, I'll tell her anyway. She gets this befuddled look on her face sometimes when I tell her scientific stuff, quite a look. Saturday, say 8:00 a.m., would that work?"

"Yes, that will be perfect, my name's Leonard Lipschitz; I didn't get yours."

"James Smythe, Mr. Lipschitz, call me Jimmy. Do you have one of those passes, seems that they are rounding up the ones not being used, so if you have one, I could park a little closer. That okay?"

"Certainly," Lipschitz wrote a note on a sheet of paper from his clipboard. "Take this to the administration building and they'll issue you a pass. You can park behind the building, I'll be looking for you at 8:00, right here, I want that stage a hundred percent perfect."

"Thanks, Mr. Lipschitz, thank you very much. All this is so exciting, can't wait to bring the missus, she will surely love the Hollywood exhibit." Davies shook Lipschitz's hand and walked over to the administration building. Five minutes later, he left with a vehicle pass that was good for the whole week, he was quite sure he would not need it after Saturday morning.

# 28

TONY WAS CONCERNED about Gini, but between the calls from the Chicago citizens more than ready to rat out their neighbors and friends, the ongoing screaming of Colonel McCormick, the finger-pointing of the Mayor, and the sad duties required by the death of his captain, he could not give her the time he thought she needed. He called her at the mayor's office the day after their night out and an unfamiliar voice answered.

"Gini Gale, please?" Alfano asked.

"Sorry, she is not in. She's taking the rest of the week off, not feeling well."

Her remark caught Alfano off-guard. "This is Detective Tony Alfano; I'm working on the bombing case per the mayor. Is His Honor in?"

"I will check, Detective."

It took longer than he thought it would, the receptionist returned finally, "He's in a meeting and he can't be disturbed."

Alfano, thinking, "Can you tell me if there are two weird looking guys in your reception area? One is thin the other is fat."

"Why, yes, they came in with Commissioner Hayden."

"Thanks, tell the mayor I'll call him later."

Alfano would have loved to sit in on that meeting, with the Tribune building still smoldering. *The political capital that will be spent after the bomber is caught is going to be huge.*

"Good morning, Sergeant, your wife, she better?"

"As good as she can be, the funeral for Tommy is this afternoon, she's had it rough these past few days."

"Yes, you're good for her."

"Thanks, some interesting things have come in."

"Give me a few minutes, then meet me at the board." Alfano sat at his desk and immediately tried to call Gini at home, no answer. After their recent incident, he was worried, she'd been through a lot, she was tough, but he still wanted to talk to her, to get her temperature and her temperament.

"What do you have?"

"The Checker cab was the one stolen from in front of Mack's Diner; it was rigged with at least fifty sticks of dynamite, according to the inspector."

"That leaves him with maybe one hundred pounds left."

"Yes, about that. No one remembers seeing the cabby as he walked through the coffee shop, so all we have is the testimony of the surviving driver."

"You believe him?"

"No reason not to, may I?"

Alfano nodded and watched as the Sergeant stuck the notes and timelines for the Tribune bombing on the cork board.

"We also looked at the shell casing and the slug from the shooting at your apartment, my guy says it was similar to what's fired by a German Mauser, the weight of the slug fits also. You were one lucky son of a bitch."

"Don't I know it, I wish I could say the same thing for Mrs. Kowalski."

"How is she doing?"

"Good, I'm going to stop by and see her later at the hospital."

"Good boy, she'll like that."

"Probably more than you know, what else you got?"

"We were lucky, the bullets that were removed from the Captain's head; they match the ones from Doyle and the Malloys. So we can assume that he was the bomber and Captain Kennedy was at the wrong place at the wrong time."

"Not going to help his family to know that, damn. He didn't need that, he was an okay guy, but this was all wrong. His wife okay?"

"It's real tough on her; she's got a funeral to deal with now. No family, no one to help her, one of the neighbors is giving her a hand. Kennedy's only brother was killed a few years back by one of the Sicilians, he got him but the guy got off a shot before he died. He was a sergeant, I knew him, a good guy."

"It feels like we're on the front lines here, McDunnah, every day it's something new."

"Last thing, we found this stuck in the bridge grate near the Captain, could be nothing, but then again, it's something, take a look at it."

The sergeant handed Alfano a piece of paper, *St Elizabeth Hospital* across the top, and *Doolittle $85.59*.

"What's this, Sarg?"

"Looks to be a receipt for some medical services at St. Elizabeth's, for a Doolittle. Was about two weeks ago, from the date on it. Strange to have found it near the Captain, but then again it could have blown in from a thousand places, you said not to let anything get by, so I had the boys collect everything. They were lucky there were holes in the bridge deck grate, got stuck in a hole a foot from the Captain's body."

"Strange, St. Elizabeth's is where Mrs. Kowalski's recovering. I'll take this with me and ask around, as you said, may be nothing or something, blown in, huh? Since I'll be out there, why not?"

"...Yeah, why not?"

Alfano tapped gently on the doorframe of Alice Kowalski's room, the second bed was empty. Harold Kowalski was not in the chair in the corner. Alice looked like hell. Her face was swollen and her shoulder was heavily bandaged, the hospital gown barely allowed a sense of modesty, as if Alice could have cared. She smiled when she saw Alfano; she waved him in with her good arm.

"Sit, sit. I understand you are my hero." Her voice was hoarse and gravelly.

"Not really, they were shooting at me and they missed, I'm the one who's sorry. They treating you okay?"

"Great and Harold's been so wonderful, all these flowers are from him, even snuck in a sausage sandwich from Andy's Deli. I didn't know how much the man loved me; he was in tears when he came to see me, so sweet."

"He does love you Alice; it's good to see you're doing well."

"Thanks, Tony, I know I've been a little bit of a pest, but I'm over it. Going home tomorrow, Harold has some time coming from the mill, maybe we'll go up to Lake Geneva, rent a cabin. Get away."

"That would be good for the two of you, a little rest, get reconnected."

"I like that, Tony. You know, I have this younger sister, I've told her all about you. She'd really like to meet you."

"Thanks, Alice, but I'm kind of seeing someone, it would be a little awkward."

"She wouldn't mind, she's the aggressive one in the family, she could really show you a good time."

"Thanks, Alice, you take care of yourself and I'll see you at home. Say hello to Harold."

Alfano quickly walked down the hall to the admissions desk, a stern-looking black-veiled nun in a broad white wimple that touched the top of her eyebrows sat at the desk. He showed the nun his shield and introduced himself.

"Yes sir, I remember you from the other night, when Mrs. Kowalski was brought in, I'm glad she is doing well. What can I do for you?"

"Well, Sister, in the course of one of our investigations, we found a receipt for your hospital's services. I'd like to show it to you and see if you remember anything about it."

"I will try, there are three of us that cover this desk and perform many other duties. We are the Poor Handmaids of Jesus Christ. We remain poor while the hospital makes a profit." She smiled at the irony.

Not sure about how to answer that, Alfano took out the receipt and handed it to the Sister.

She removed a ledger book from the small collection of ledgers on the desk and started paging through the originals.

"Yes here it is, I remember it very well, a young boy was carried in by a well-dressed man, quite handsome for an old gentleman, if you ask me, but what do I know. They were followed by a distraught woman in her mid-thirties. The child had fallen from his bicycle and hit his head, we examined the child, other than a bump and a scrape, he was fine. He spent the night here and then went home. The gentleman paid for everything, quite a proper man, very polite as well and quite deferential to us, often not the case for non-Catholics."

"He wasn't Catholic?"

"Quite certain, mentioned it in passing, but he did say that he had great respect. Mrs. Doolittle, now she …"

"Mrs. Doolittle?"

"Oh yes, the woman, her name was Doolittle and the boy was her son. He was quite the rogue for a seven-year-old, if I say so myself. Very proper, polite, said thank you and yes ma'am at every opportunity. I thought that he might be related to the gentleman, maybe his grandson, their manners were quite similar. Mrs. Doolittle said that he was a friend that lived in the same building."

Alfano could not believe his luck. "By chance, do you have her address?"

"Of course I do, Detective. But I see from the appointment book, she will be here in an hour for a quick follow-up; maybe you can see her then. It might save you some trouble."

"Thank you, Sister, is there somewhere where I can get a cup of coffee?"

"Down that hall to the end, then turn right, it's not the best but will suffice, or so I've been told."

While he made notes in a third notebook, Alfano cooled his heels in the cafeteria. The coffee wasn't all that bad, but he was delighted with the oatmeal cookie. Sixty-five minutes later, an attractive woman walked into the room, followed by a handsome, well-dressed boy. She headed directly to Alfano.

"Excuse me, are you Detective Alfano? The nun said you wished to talk with me. Is everything all right?"

Alfano stood up as she approached, he looked at the boy. "May I buy you a cup of coffee and a pop for the boy?"

"Ralph, would you like a pop?"

He nodded.

"And yes, a cup of coffee would be nice, Detective. But what's this all about?"

"One minute." Alfano allowed the pair to relax while he purchased their beverages. He carried them to the table. "There you are. How old are you, Ralph?"

"...Seven, sir."

"Seven, you are certainly big for your age. And are you feeling okay?"

"Yes, sir, the doctor said I'm as fit as a fiddle, but I need to be more careful riding my bike."

"Always a good idea." He turned to Mrs. Doolittle. "I understand a gentleman brought Ralph in when he had his tumble a few weeks back."

"Yes, Mr. Smythe, he lives upstairs. Why?"

Alfano ignored the question, "Do you know Mr. Smythe's first name?"

"Yes, it is James. You still haven't answered my question."

"How long has Mr. Smythe lived in the building?"

"Two years. I won't answer any more questions until you tell me why you are asking them." She pulled Ralph closer to her and stared at Alfano.

He took a deep breath; he was about to begin when a man walked into the cafeteria. He was wearing a tweed jacket, a bold red bow tie, and two-toned shoes. When he saw Alfano sitting with Mrs. Doolittle, he turned back toward the door and began to run.

# 29

ALFANO COULDN'T BELIEVE his eyes when he saw Smythe enter the cafeteria, he was stunned. And when Smythe disappeared, he excused himself and quickly followed; he watched as the man disappeared out the front doors near admissions. By this time, Alfano was also running. He couldn't believe how fast the older man could move. Just outside the doors, he scanned the parking lot and saw a black Ford Model B heading toward the Western Avenue entry at a smart clip. When the Model B hit the street, Alfano could hear the engine rev through the gears as it headed north toward North Avenue.

He had parked the Packard at the drop-off. Twenty seconds later, he was heading up Western Avenue. When he pushed the pedal to the floor, the engine's sudden acceleration stunned him, the car began to fishtail, within a hundred feet he was in control. He watched Smythe fly through the North Avenue intersection and continue north. When Alfano reached the street, he got jammed behind a delivery truck and had to swerve left to pass it; he scared a man in an old Model T making the turn onto North. Alfano saw Smythe's car weaving back and forth four blocks ahead, he was heading toward Milwaukee Avenue. Alfano downshifted to slow down but did not touch the brake, then he upshifted, the car sped up but did not swerve or fishtail. He saw the Ford turn right on Milwaukee. At Bloomingdale, he cut east, hoping to catch Smythe as he headed south on Milwaukee. He waited thirty seconds for the black Ford, but it never showed. He slowly turned northwest on Milwaukee and paralleled the "L," looking for Smythe and the Coupe. Halfway up Milwaukee, he turned back under the elevated tracks on Oakley Avenue, he still came up blank. At Winnebago, he turned back to parallel the tracks, as he approached Western Avenue, he almost drove past the car before he spotted it. *Damn, he turned down Winnebago, not Milwaukee, damn it.*

Alfano reached the Ford and pulled the Packard to a stop in the street; the Ford sat tight against the opposite curb, he drew his pistol. Focused on the car, Alfano started to approach the vehicle when a delivery truck came right toward him, horn blaring. He took a step back and waved the truck past. At that exact second, the Ford exploded, throwing Detroit steel and gasoline across the street and sidewalk. Luckily, he was in the shadow of the truck and its rear wheels at that moment. Mrs. Alfano's detective son would have been playing patty-cake with the angels had he been any closer.

The car burned hot and steadily until the fire department put it out. No one was hurt. The driver of the passing truck was fortunate; he was seated on the opposite side of the cab, away from the blast. Unfortunately the truck's cargo, a load of Coca-Cola, was shattered; it filled the gutters of North Winnebago Avenue.

Every eight to ten minutes, the "L" rattled overhead. The noise clued Alfano into Smythe's probable escape route after setting the timer or fuse on the bomb.

The Packard had a few superficial wounds; the truck had shielded the car quite well. After an hour of conversation with the local cops, he got a strange visit to the scene from Commissioner Hayden. Four reporters followed the commissioner like a pack of dogs looking for a bone, apparently, Hayden thought it necessary to publicly congratulate him for finding the bomber. Alfano responded, "Does it look like I caught the fucking bomber?" Pissed at all the politics Alfano drove the few blocks to the Doolittle apartment.

Alfano rang the bell and Ralph opened the door.

"Mr. Alfano, I don't think my mother wants to see you. She told me to tell you to go away."

"I understand, but I think she needs to hear me and talk to me because that's what adults do. When we have problems, we talk about them. And I have a problem that only your mother can help with. So please ask her, I'll wait right here." Alfano backed away from the door, reducing the threat to the boy and his home. He walked to the sidewalk and lit a cigarette. He could still smell the acrid smoke of the burnt Ford on his clothes.

His back was to the screen door when he heard it squeak open, Mrs. Doolittle, a little red-eyed, stood in the doorway.

"Detective, how can I help you?"

"Mrs. Doolittle, I have a real problem and you are the only person in the whole world who can help me. It seems that Mr. James Smythe, your fellow resident and friend, is the man I am looking for."

"Why? What has he done?"

"I have reason to believe that he is the man who has been blowing up buildings and killing people since May Day, twenty-five days ago. Many people have died from the explosions and several have been directly murdered by Mr. Smythe. It's my job to find him, maybe, with your help, he won't be able to hurt anyone else ever again."

"I don't believe you, Mr. Smythe is not that kind of man. He is kind and generous; he helped us when Ralph was hurt; he has even helped us when times were tight. I don't believe you one bit."

"Do you know where he was last week when the Democratic Ward offices were bombed?"

"He was in Springfield, he's a farm equipment salesman and he said the trip was profitable."

Alfano hated to do this; the man had so beguiled her and wrapped the two of them in his fantasy, it would be difficult for her to believe anything, otherwise. He shook his head, "Sorry to say this, but he was right here, staying at the Drake Hotel, Mrs. Doolittle."

"I don't believe you."

"I saw him, I know he was there, we have witnesses."

Alfano heard the screen door open; Ralph walked to his mother's side and took her hand.

"Why are you doing this to my mother?" Ralph asked. "Mr. Smythe is my friend, he bought me a bicycle, when I broke it, he bought me another. He helped me when I was hurt and now you say he's a bad man. He is not a bad man."

"Ralph, sometimes people are not who they say they are, they are hiding from something or someone. And that's what Mr. Smythe is doing, he's hiding. Mrs. Doolittle, I will have to look in Mr. Smythe's room. I don't have a warrant, but I can get one. But time is critical. Will you let me have a look?"

"Detective, I can't stop you, like him, I rent; the owner lives in Glenview. So do what you must, I'm sure you'll realize that this is all a mistake."

Alfano slipped by Mrs. Doolittle and climbed the stairs to Smythe's room. He tried the handle, it was locked. Alfano wasn't sure if Smythe had booby-trapped the door to his room since he'd just dealt with the Ford Coupe explosion. Then he looked down the stairs and saw Ralph. *Of course, he wouldn't have, it would be too dangerous for Ralph and his mother. The man might kill them if he miscalculated.*

Alfano slammed his shoulder into the wooden door,

breaking the locks away from the frame. Nothing exploded. He went deliberately through the room, it was neat, orderly, everything in its place, the ashtray held three cigarette butts, all PLAYERS. When he went into the bedroom, he was stunned by the paraphernalia that was spread across the desk, two alarm clocks sat to the left, other bits and gears sat in tightly organized groups, three coils of wires, red, black, and green to the right with rolls of black cloth tape amongst them. Numerous pliers, clippers, and small screwdrivers populated the remainder of the desk. An ashtray, almost filled to its limit, sat to the far right. An empty box with the face of a British sailor sat next to it, *PLAYERS* across the top.

"Oh my God," Mrs. Doolittle said from the door of the bedroom. "All of this is his?"

"Yes, everything you see here can be used to make timers that can explode dynamite. Does he have a garage nearby?"

"Yes, out back, he keeps his car there."

"I don't think it's there now. Excuse me, I don't see a phone in his rooms, may I use yours?"

Mrs. Doolittle stood aside and watched as Alfano went down the stairs to her apartment, she had left the door open. The phone sat in an alcove in the hallway.

"McDunnah, Alfano here. You got the word already, yeah I'm fine, not a scratch. But I'm in the bomber's apartment, exactly where we thought it would be." Alfano gave the address. "Have the boys come up here and take a good look around and collect everything, photos, prints, everything and for God's sake don't let the press hear of it. There's a woman and a boy here that know nothing concrete about the man, they know him as James Smythe, the same name we have. Still don't believe that's his real name. I'm going to check the garage out back where he kept his car. As I told the boys back at the explosion, he probably jumped the "L," he could be anywhere. I'll be in later."

Alfano searched the garage thoroughly and found nothing. He had to have another place, somewhere nearby, somewhere he could walk to. Alfano guessed Smythe would be headed there to lay low. He also wondered what Smythe intended to do with the remaining hundred pounds of dynamite. *What or where is your next target, you son of a bitch?*

# 30

DAVIES HEADED DOWNTOWN toward the tangle of elevated "L's" that joined near the heart of the city. Once there, he could move in any direction and, at least for a while, he could disappear. It had been foolish to go to the hospital; he knew that now. He had wanted to see how the boy and Mrs. Doolittle were fairing. So much to take care of, no man to help her, he was glad to help but he'd be no help to her now. *Alfano is probably in my apartment; he'll find the timers and the odds and ends of my craft.* He knew he could always buy more; he was never a man to collect things or put stock in memories with trinkets and toys. There was nothing there to mourn its loss, nothing. He stopped by the Central Post Office, there was one letter addressed to him.

*Dear Mr. Smythe,*
*I understand all the difficulties you are going through, I sincerely do. But we must continue to move forward with the plan. Saturday is critical to the contract and its purpose. Through you, Saturday will be my day of vengeance. You will receive your final payment on Sunday morning. I know you will succeed, and those that have sinned will be punished.*
*Sincerely . . . .*

No signature, he'd never considered the sex of his client until that moment; he'd always thought it was a man, someone powerful in City Hall with a reason for vengeance and retribution. Now he wasn't sure, there was a stern tenderness to the note. He bought a new sports coat and a hat and gave the old items to a man in a soup kitchen line. He removed his bow tie and walked across Chicago's Loop with an open shirt, the weather was mild, but a storm was forecast. He stopped at a small diner and ordered breakfast, even though it was late in the day.

He hid in the crush of the late afternoon commute, thousands jammed the trains, many were transferring from the Clark Street "L." The Cubs had played a game at Wrigley and at five o'clock, the happy fans with a win against the Boston Braves, blended in with the mix of employees heading home. He headed north on the Blue Line that paralleled Milwaukee and left the train at North Avenue. From there, he headed to his rented garage and spent ten minutes walking the neighborhood, looking for cops or patrol cars. He saw a few driving east and west on North Avenue, but none stopped. By the time he reached the garage, it was dark, no one saw him slip through the door. He poured himself a glass of whiskey, lit a cigarette and took stock, breathing easy for the first time since escaping the hospital.

Luckily he had moved the final assemblies of the clocks to the garage earlier that morning while Mrs. Doolittle was at work. He was sad about the loss of the Ford Coupe, it was a magnificent piece of engineering and he had enjoyed owning it, now, like everything else in his life, it was a memory, nothing more. He never intended to drive it to California. He walked around the panel truck and picked at a few pieces of tape that remained stuck along the trim. Looking closely, he was impressed with the lettering he had done and how closely it matched the real painter's trucks. He was glad that no one had looked too closely when he went through the fair, it would have been embarrassing to see masking tape still stuck on the company truck. He would not be leaving the garage until it was time to move the truck to the fair, that would be about 7:00 a.m. on Saturday, about thirty-six hours to wait. *Friday night will be a long night*; he crawled into his cot and turned down the lamp to a mere flicker. No electricity, no strong lights, nothing bright until the next day, the day he would finish building the last two bombs.

Alfano was at his wits' end. He'd had the bomber in his hands and the man had given him the slip, lost, blending in with the millions living in Chicago. For the rest of the evening, Alfano drove through the neighborhoods around Smythe's apartment. He knew the chances were slim that he'd find him, but it gave him something to do while he thought everything through; what drove the man, why use dynamite, why the random deaths? But he also wanted to apprehend the person or persons behind Smythe paying him to blow up buildings and kill people. Maybe no one else was involved but after twenty-two years of looking into the dark souls of men and women, he knew he was right. *There is someone directing Mr. Smythe, my Mr. Suave, someone must be pulling his strings.*

When it was too dark to see his surroundings clearly, he returned to the Racine Station, Sergeant McDunnah was waiting for him.

"Jesus, Mary, and Joseph, Detective, I can't wait until we get two-way radios in the cars, I've been waiting with this for three hours."

"Well, I'm home now Mother, what do you have?"

"We got lucky again, there were fingerprints at the apartment and we matched them, how the hell they did it so quickly I don't know, but a match came up. His prints had been set aside by the FBI in Washington."

"Sometimes you're lucky, what did you find?"

"This fella's a piece of work. His real name is Garon Lloyd Davies, American-born but folks were Welsh, lived in Pennsylvania for a while, then Denver, then he went missing for some years, now he's here. Was a demolitions man, handled dynamite in the mines and for others who needed his services in Colorado, did roads and some tunnel work. As I said, he's been missing for years, no one I talked to knew where he was. Now he shows up here."

"Someone's paying him, I know it. That's the link. But what's the end game here? Is he done yet? If not, what's he going to do with the remaining dynamite? There's enough left to take down a fucking skyscraper or a bridge, or a *FAIR*."

Sergeant McDunnah said the word at the same time. "Jesus, Mary, and Joseph. If that's his intention, he could kill hundreds or even thousands. We need to stop it, to prevent the opening until we can go through the whole fair grounds and make sure that he hasn't already placed the bomb or bombs, God forbid. You have to call the mayor and stop it; the fair opens the day after tomorrow."

Alfano ran his fingers through his thick black hair, how long that would last was a matter of conjecture, at this rate, he'd pull it out before it turned gray. "The Mayor won't stop this, not on my say so, there's too much riding on it for the city. If he delays the opening, the rest of the big cities will piss on him like he was on fire, not a chance. I've got this hunch that whoever is behind this is already in City Hall. Someone wants the Mayor to fail; someone wants the city to fail."

"I've had that same eerie feeling; this isn't some crackpot, some nut." "This has been a methodical process since day one, each bomb targeted a branch of the government or business, each bomb was an attempt to punish and expose them."

"I agree with you, this goes deeper, it's extremely personal. One sociopath finds another and the repercussions roll through the city like a firestorm. Something set this off, something was the catalyst." Alfano walked to the cork board, McDunnah had placed more notes on the board, one *St. Elizabeth's*, another *Mrs. Doolittle*, one had Smythe/Davies address inscribed and there was a pin stuck on the map for the location of his apartment.

"Sergeant, find me the schedule for Saturday's events at the fair. Somebody downtown must have it."

"Don't have to, it was in this morning's paper." Sergeant McDunnah retrieved a copy of the *Tribune*. He opened it to the section that said *Century of Progress Fair* across the header, a column of copy interspersed with photos filled the page. The schedule for Saturday and Sunday's events was outlined with a box.

"*Saturday's opening is at Soldier Field, all the dignitaries will be there, starts with a parade down Michigan Avenue to the field,*" McDunnah read. "Big doings from I can see. I know that every patrolman not on duty has been called in. Going to be quite something. Do you think our man might try to do something?"

"Can only be it, once you blow up the Tribune what else is there? Wrigley Field, Comiskey Park, I don't think so, they are not political, this has politics written all over it. Hell, until a few days ago, FDR himself was going to be here to open the fair. So everybody who is anybody in the world of Illinois politics will be there, along with maybe a hundred thousand other folks. If you're going to blow something or somebody up you, couldn't have a better audience for your vengeance."

"How do we go about it?"

"I'm going downtown. Call the mayor's office and tell them I have to talk to him right away. Tell them I will be there in twenty minutes."

Laurel and Hardy weren't in the mayor's waiting room this time. An older woman was sitting in Gini's chair; Alfano had never met her. She had a severe, stern look about her; Alfano could tell she had taken on the job of guard dog with authority.

"The Mayor in?" Alfano asked.

"He will buzz me when he is available."

"Is he in?" When he saw her take a quick look at the door, he knew the mayor was in his office.

Alfano leaned over and put two fists on the edge of the desk, "Here's the skinny, in about ten seconds, I'm going through that door. You can buzz me through with that little button under the desk or you can watch me bust it down. Either way, in fifteen seconds I'm going to be talking with him. Now counting, one, two, three, ..."

At four, the woman looked at the door, closed her eyes and pushed the button. A loud buzz reverberated around the room. Alfano pushed the door open.

In *flagrante delicto* was the first thing that jumped into his head when he saw the mayor and a very cute, very young lady ensconced comfortably on his lap, a smear of lipstick brightened his right cheek.

"What the fuck do you think you're doing, Alfano?"

"Get her out of here your honor, and I mean right now."

She needed no encouragement, within seconds, she had gathered up and rebuttoned much of her wardrobe and scooted out the second door to the office. Her fragrance remained.

"Damn it, Alfano, I'll have you licking the horse stalls clean after I'm done with you."

"I don't fucking care. I'm here to save your worthless political Irish hide, sir."

"Get out!"

"In due time, you listen for a few minutes. Can I offer you a glass of whiskey, maybe a cigar? I've got a story to tell."

Fifteen minutes later, all the mayor could say was, "Holy shit. What do you suggest now?"

"Shut it down, the opening festivities."

"…Won't happen."

"I know, but we need to inspect everything and everyone. No one comes or goes without checking them first, especially the people working the fair. He's very good at getting in and out of places right under our noses."

"That's impossible, we can't check *everyone* and the first hint that there's a bomb somewhere on the fairgrounds is the same as saying we're closed, we're done, we're fucked. This has to be kept quiet, very quiet."

"Understood. Do you trust Hayden?"

"Hayden, sure, why not? I know you two have issues, but he's a good boy."

"Well, I think someone inside city hall is behind all this. Someone is passing on information–that's why I was shot at. No one knows where I live outside of my department. Some-one here could get to my files and pass on my address. So I'm not sure about Hayden."

"Alfano, you may not like me but personally, I don't give a fuck. But I'm a politician, I've watched people for years and I can tell when they're right or wrong or crooked. Hayden has his faults, his foibles, but he's okay. He's had plenty of opportunities to knife me in the back in big ways, public ways, and he hasn't. I strongly believe he's not the guy. It's got to be someone else."

"It's your ass, if you pardon me, Mayor. Get Hayden to move heaven and earth to watch over what's going on at the fair. Check on the workers, especially after midnight on Friday night."

"Why after midnight?"

"Davies uses mechanical clocks to set off his bombs, sim-ple and effective. But he has a twelve-hour window to work with. He likes to set his clocks and watch from far away. So if he's going to blow up the opening ceremonies, his timers need to be set after midnight."

Mayor Kelly stood there looking at Anthony Alfano for about ten seconds, nothing was said. He reached for the intercom button, "Miss Abernathy, please get Commissioner Hayden and Mr. Nash on the phone."

As Alfano drove back to the Racine Station, he couldn't get Gini out of his head. *Why was she out? Why didn't she answer her phone? She seemed well last night until the garbage truck disturbed her.* He understood, his heart went out to her but why the sudden disappearance. He missed her very much.

# 31

DAVIS LICKED the envelope and sealed it. He placed it in his coat pocket; he would drop it in a mailbox on the way to the fair. As he pushed it into his jacket pocket, he felt a piece of paper, the last note from his client. *Sincerely* kept running around in his head, he couldn't stop thinking about it. He placed the tool chest on the workbench; it was a simple ruse, a smaller metal case inside the larger tool chest. This would allow him to retain the larger painter's tool chest after placing the smaller case under the stage. He had placed paintbrushes and other incidentals on top of the smaller case. His pistol lay hidden under the smaller case. He had to be prepared if they were searching employees and craftsmen. Everything was set, a switch on the smaller case was held in place with black cloth electrical tape, insuring his safety. When the time was right, all he would have to do is peel back the tape and throw the toggle. The bomb would be in the unstoppable hands of time after that.

He opened the back of the panel truck; two large wooden paint boxes were secured to the floor of the truck along with the smaller padlocked tool chest containing the battery and alarm clock mechanisms. Additional paint cans, some empty, were placed next to the boxes. A canvas tarp speckled with paint was laid over everything. Unseen wires led from the tool chest to the two wooden 'paint' crates. His goal, after the truck was parked in its final location, was to secure it from prying eyes and curious hands the best way he knew how, the huge padlock on the back double-doors would do the job just fine.

He looked at his watch, 9:30 p.m. He poured another glass of courage and lit a cigarette. If all went well, he would be heading to California in twenty-four hours.

Alfano nodded off in the Packard, even the noise from the workers inside the fair wasn't enough to prevent him from falling asleep. By his count, he'd been up almost thirty hours straight since his visit to Mrs. Kowalski. That was always the way it worked, a slow slog collecting clues and taking interviews, the pace builds, names are found, actions are foreseen, people confess, bad people get arrested. But every case was different and this one was more difficult than all the rest. No one had confessed, actions were coming, things he hadn't planned for and he was missing a name. He woke with a start; the cigarette had burned to his fingers.

He got out of the car and stretched, he needed sleep, but he couldn't push himself away. The next twenty-four hours would tell all. Would he be right? Would there be vengeance for the deaths of Eddy and Adele Doyle and all the others Davies had killed? Would he be the hand of vengeance, for the dead and maimed, that would lay Davies down?

A patrol car pulled up to Alfano, the rain put a sheen over everything, making things look smooth and glossy.

"Go home, Detective," McDunnah said. "There's nothing to see here, get some sleep, you will need it tomorrow. My best guess, he'll do nothing until then. He's in no hurry; the speeches don't start until after 10:00 a.m., two hours after the park opens. So go home and get some sleep, I'll make sure one of the boys calls you at 5:00 a.m., will that work?"

Alfano knew McDunnah was right, there was nothing he could do, for now. "Thank you, Mother, tell you what, the station's closer – I'll bunk on the cot in the holding cell, call me there."

"Will do, goodnight Detective."

"Goodnight, Sergeant, be careful."

"Always am." McDunnah rolled up the window and slowly drove toward the north entry gate of the fair, a low-key command center, such as it was, had been set up in a dark green army surplus tent in the small lot behind the administration building.

Alfano pulled up to the curb in front of the station house, the rain, more of a nuisance than anything, continued to fall. The weather called for a drizzly wet opening day. All the planning and all money thrown into this 427-acre spot along the Lake Michigan shoreline couldn't stop Mother Nature from doing her best to piss on the whole venture.

Alfano stood at the cork board and looked at the pictures and labels and pins. The text: *Century of Progress,* stood out. *What will change in the next century? Where will I be in twenty years? What will the Century of Progress Fair look like in 2033? Ray guns and rocket ships, devices for sending pictures over phone lines, real lie detectors, tell who someone is by just taking their picture, personal radios kept in your pocket, instant communications anywhere in the world?* He didn't know or care, he walked back to the cell and laid his head on the pillow of the hard mattress.

"What!?" Alfano yelled as he was violently shaken. McDunnah's mug was staring him in the face.

"When you fall asleep, you sleep like the dead. It's 5:00 a.m.; we need to get going. The last of the contractors left at about 2:00, there's maybe two or three hundred returning at 6:00 to put the spit and polish to anything that was missed. The rain makes it difficult, but as they say, 'The show must go on!'"

"Who the hell said that?"

"I haven't a fucking clue." McDunnah shoved a mug of coffee in front of Alfano.

"Don't know whether to drink it or throw it on my face."

"Let me choose."

Garon Davies opened the top of the mailbox, took a look at the address and dropped the envelope inside. The drizzle had let up, but the temperature remained cool. He'd spent the early morning transforming himself. He sported thick sideburns with an Irish flare about them. He'd shaved his thin mustache and now wore a thicker, more robust style replacement stuck on with spirit glue. He'd even darkened his skin a touch with brown shoe polish to disguise the pasty face he'd acquired during the winter. He couldn't wait to start his California tan, one that would be at least three shades darker than the makeup he'd recently applied. Davies also altered his clothing but kept the same jacket. He was wearing workman-like, thick pants with a couple of patches on them, his fedora, once stylish, now sported a hole and a worn brim. His shoes were a far cry from the two-toned Florsheims. He was glad that the clothes were clean and lice-free.

As he drove through the Chicago streets in the early morning, there was an unusual bustle about, cars and trucks seemed to be stacked at each intersection as he headed south on Western, most were headed east. He knew the parade would start somewhere near the Drake Hotel on Michigan then head south. He paralleled the route south on Western Avenue then turned east toward the fair on Roosevelt Road; at State Street, he went south to the Cermak and came in through the 22nd Street entry. Two police cars waited at the entry. He showed them the pass that Lipschitz had helped him acquire. When asked where he was headed, he simply said, "The Ford Building, some finishing up to do, busy day, boys, very busy." They waved him through.

Sitting behind Davies, three trucks back, idling in the damp air off the lake, Anthony Alfano waited in his Packard. He watched the trucks ahead of him turn left and right as they entered, none stood out to him or seemed out of place. In fact, he recognized the Otto Spellbinder truck; he'd seen their vehicles around Chicago for years. He was pleased to see they were still in business, considering the collapse of the building industry in the city. *Nice truck, bright, shiny.*

He turned and followed the Spellbinder truck along Columbus Drive; it slowed and then parked in front of the Ford building. As he passed the truck, he noticed that the driver took that moment to turn away from the street and look toward the building. Alfano continued on to the administration building. McDunnah was already there, so was Commissioner Hayden.

Hayden didn't look happy, "What the hell's going on, Alfano, the mayor has been jumping through hoops, doing a fucking Irish jig over your assumptions. You sure this guy will be here?"

"Yeah, he'll be here. It's the only game left in town, the only big time play. Everything else was practice for today. Your men ready?"

"As ready as can be, Detective," McDunnah said. "Was hard to find the additional men, so many are assigned to the parade. We've been able to add forty men to the fair security task force, they have been told to look for anything suspicious and call us here if they see anything. They have also been told to do nothing until we clear it."

"Your bomb expert here, Commissioner?"

"Yes, he's good, very good. Got through the gang and taxi wars, so either he's good or he's very lucky."

"Let's hope both."

This was the first time Alfano was on the fair's property; he was impressed. The overcast was disappointing but the bright colors and the sharp edge of the architecture seemed to be a pleasant departure from the architecture of the city, including the urban architecture heavily influenced by the Columbian Exposition more than thirty-five years earlier. There was an upward spirit surrounding the buildings, with their towers and columns. The two most dramatic structures were the 628 foot-tall towers of the Sky Ride. These two steel towers, looking like giant erector set monstrosities anchored both sides of the fair. The cables and cars hung between them split the fair across the long lagoon. Even this early in the morning, he could see the aluminum rocket ship cars that traveled from tower to tower, taking people higher than they had ever been in their lives. Alfano imagined that it was probably like flying.

Great concrete columns rose up the inside of each tower; in each, four elevators rose to the spaceships and the observation deck, each rocket could carry thirty people. These sentinels were the tallest structures in Chicago providing a stunning view of four states. For Alfano, the Rockets made his stomach queasy, the thought of being up that high made him very uneasy.

"Let's take a look at the speaker's platform," Alfano said as he pushed open the flap of the tent, the rain started in earnest.

"Give it a few minutes, Detective, we can check it when it gets a little brighter outside," Hayden said.

"I'll give you fifteen, then we go."

Alfano stood under an awning that was set up next to the tent and smoked a cigarette. More trucks and cars passed by and then the Otto Spellbinder truck went through the turn-around at the north entry, he watched it head south, the truck turned into the parking lot in front of the Field Museum and disappeared. Then, to Alfano's surprise, another Spellbinder truck passed by, heading north, followed by one of the ultra-modern buses used to transport people around the fair. He tried to imagine what the roads and drives would look like when they were filled with thousands of people.

An administrative aide approached Alfano. "Detective, all the contractors are required to be out of the fairgrounds by 8:00, unless otherwise authorized; the fair opens at 8:30. Only those with a special permit are allowed to remain and that has to be posted on their dashboard."

"Your name is?"

"Lipschitz, Leonard Lipschitz. I'm in charge of coordinating the opening ceremonies, this rain is disappointing."

"Isn't it, has anything strange happened during the last few days, anything that stands out?"

"Other than trying to get ready for a huge party with 40,000 guests, no, nothing really stands out. It's been the usual craziness the last two months, but almost everything is ready. It is going to be an exciting summer."

"Right now, I don't need excitement."

"Pardon me? No one has told me why there is a sudden interest by the police in the opening ceremonies; we have had numerous meetings and liaisons with the Chicago police, probably hundreds. Is there something more I should know?"

"No, sonny boy, no," Hayden said. "We are just here to help. You know, just City Hall holding hands with the fair. We have a lot invested in this as well."

Unconvinced by Hayden's explanation, Lipschitz walked out of the tent quickly and headed across the parking lot to the administration building.

"That was awfully politic of you, Frank, I've never seen you that easy before," Alfano said.

"It was the truth and this son of a bitch scares the hell out of me."

# 32

DAVIES WATCHED as the Packard continued past him and disappeared around the curve of the road. He was certain it was Alfano; he could recognize that car anywhere. *But how the hell did he know I'd be here.* He knew the man was good, that's why the client wanted him dead, this just proved that they knew what to expect from a man with Alfano's skills. But Davies also knew the fair was huge, in fact, when the people started coming in it at 8:30 a.m., it would be relatively easy to get lost in the hundreds of buildings and hallways on the grounds. Parking the truck was the first requirement. Next he knew we had to get it into position near the tower, set the device and then move on to the stage. Set it and forget it, the client was brilliant. He drove north, past the administration building, then he doubled back to the far end of Soldier Field. Three contractor's trucks were parked in the small lot near the building; he slipped the panel truck next to the steel and concrete base of the west tower. The whole parking area was hidden from the public; directly across the plaza, hundreds would line the walks in front of the Hall of Science. He looked up into the steel structure and then followed the cables to the far tower, 1,800 feet away. He could see four of the rocket cars moving between the towers. He walked to the back of the truck and opened the doors, removed the tool chest, and set it on the paving. After a quick look around, he peeled back the canvas and unlocked the second tool chest. The clock mechanism was functioning; the ticking was reassuring. He looked at the wires and gently tugged on them to ensure that they were connected. He knew his baby-girls were asleep, when they woke up, no one would sleep for days. He rechecked the timers, they were in order. He closed the lid and slipped the padlock through the hasp, pulled the tarp over everything, took one more look, closed the doors and locked the larger padlock. Satisfied, he realized that it had stopped raining, he smiled just for a second. Within thirty seconds, he had crossed the service road, entered Soldier Field Stadium and disappeared.

Alfano walked out to the promenade that surrounded the lagoons; maybe a dozen people were out and about, most were collecting papers and bits of refuse, some carried brooms. The rain had freshened up the crispness of the architecture but muted some of the colors of the buildings; he would be back when it was sunny.

"What do you think?" McDunnah said. "In an hour, this placed will be mobbed, thousands are waiting at the gates already."

"I think I hate waiting, he's here, I can feel him," Alfano said. "Let me ask you something. What would you do if you were Davies? What would you target? Your guess and mine are as good as anyone's, if in fact, maybe better since we've been hanging around criminals most of our lives. The drive here is vengeance; this is all new, there's nothing here with a past. What has a past, McDunnah?"

"Mostly people, they are the past and future, everything we do set's us up for the next minute, the next day. People cause pain; their actions can cause a need for vengeance in someone's mind."

"So what person or persons could cause this much hatred and require this foul need for vengeance?"

"Other than some bankers and lawyers, it would have to be politicians. Especially in this town, Lord knows they have their fingers in every pie and if it's not in their hand, they're not in the game. An empty politician's palm is a sad thing, don't you think?"

"McDunnah, don't get me started, yeah politicians, and in a few hours we will have a hundred of the state's finest here, from the Governor all the way down to the lowest alderman."

"You're being redundant."

"Yeah, I guess I am. If there are scores to settle for the past few years, they have to be with the politicians in this town. Some say Cermak was the first when he was shot and others would follow, the Democrat's make him out to be a hero, saved the president and all, others say it was revenge for Nitti. Vengeance and revenge start from the same place, in the soul, and those motives have been with us for tens of thousands of years."

"*Vengeance is mine*, Romans 12:19."

"Sometimes people want to give God a hand and try to move the process along. I think it's a woman, a very rich woman, someone with a place at the political table, a wife, a rich girlfriend, a spurned lover."

"Maybe, a woman fits the profile. A man would be more direct, less involved with the intrigue and theater we've seen unfold."

"Yes, women savor and men slaughter."

"I like it. What do we do?" McDunnah said as he lit Alfano's cigarette.

"In a few hours, all the politicians will be in the stadium, sitting on the dais, all lined up like ducks in a shooting gallery. Somewhere nearby there's a bomb waiting to do God's work. That's where we'll find it."

"All hundred pounds of it? Hell, five sticks would reorganize the Democratic Party in this town for twenty years. ... The rest?"

"Somewhere else on the fairgrounds, somewhere that will shake the foundation of the whole system, industry, automobile companies and government." For a moment, the sun cracked the gray ceiling and sunlight danced on the waters of the lagoon and reflected off the shiny rocket cars slowly coursing their way from west to east. "That's where I'd go, nothing would make a louder statement than taking down those towers."

"Tony, you really think so? Strap a hundred pounds of dynamite around one of those beasts, it would be pretty obvious."

"How about from the inside, in one of the elevators?"

"Possible, but that's a good-sized box or two, someone's bound to see it. Wonder where it is."

"A disguise, it's in something innocuous, simple, an everyday thing."

They both turned toward the towers as a truck backfired; both men jumped and started to laugh.

"Jesus, we on edge or what?"

"No kidding, but look, it's right in front of us. Trucks are everywhere today, tomorrow, no trucks. We know Davies repainted his Ford, that was obvious after he blew up his car. Red paint under black, he has the tools and a place to do all this. Altering a truck, it would be easy for him, mix it in among the other contractors, then wait. ...But when?"

"If one bomb goes off before the other, they will shut this place down, there will be panic this town's never seen," McDunnah added. "No one in and no one out."

"He has to watch, he always stays nearby to see it happen. Like the kid who saw him the night of the Polk bombing, he waited almost an hour to see it go off. No, I think he'll set them and then stay around, blend in, and watch for the big bang."

"Where do we start?"

"The stage, tell your men to keep an eye out for anything suspicious. I don't think he'll make a mistake; he's too cool for that. So we search and see what we can find."

"And hope we have the time to look."

# 33

DAVIES WALKED briskly across the damp grass of the playing field toward the large stage set up for the opening ceremonies. In a few hours, tens of thousands of Chicagoans, tourists, and visitors would begin filling the stands. He had ten minutes to get in, set the bomb and leave. The stage would be destroyed along with everyone standing on it, the blast would cause some damage outward, but most of the damage would be directed upward.

As he approached the stage, he saw Leonard Lipschitz.

"Excuse me, are you Mr. Lipschitz?"

"Yes, can I help you?"

"The name is Smythe, my brother said I should talk to you."

"Your brother?"

"Yes, the other day, he talked with you about helping you this morning, tying up any loose ends. Well, he asked me to take his place, he's under the weather if you know what I mean, and I could use the money."

"I'm too busy to find you something to do now, just go away."

"Just a little something, anything. I see that the tarps aren't set right around the stage there, I could straighten them, sir.

And clean up over there."

Three other people were walking toward Lipschitz; he didn't need their interference, more problems. "Sure, Smythe, fix the tarps and clean up. Just get out of my hair, okay?"

"Thank ye, thank ye. I'll do a right fine job." Davies immediately headed toward the stage, carrying his tool chest. A minute later, he disappeared behind the backdrop; in seconds, he had wormed his way halfway under the boards. The awning over the temporary stage kept the ground relatively dry. Under the center of the stage, near one of the posts, he found the ideal location. Cross bracing led to a narrow shelf that was out of sight at a glance. He opened the case and removed the brushes and the tape; he pulled the smaller case out and gently set it on the grass. He pulled out the revolver and slipped it inside the waistband of his pants as a precaution. Next, he turned the case so the switch was easy to reach, then lifted and set the box on the ledge and secured it with three wraps of tape. He put the brushes back in the larger tool chest and closed it. Davies took one more look around, peeled back the tape, took a deep breath and switched on the bomb.

*Coffee*, all he could think of was *coffee*. Davies left the area behind the stage, tool chest in hand, and walked slowly toward one of the first concession stands he spied. The large clock over the administration building indicated the time as 8:12, seventeen minutes until the fair's first visitors.

"Coffee ma'am, please and one of those crullers, if you don't mind."

"...Mind? Glory be, isn't this exciting," the woman said. "I have been waiting for this day for two years, ever since I won one of the contracts to open a concession. You must be proud of your work, sir, very proud. Isn't this all just so wonderful?" She put a mug of coffee on the counter and a glazed cruller on a plate. "Make yourself comfortable because in about ten minutes the whole world will be coming to this counter."

"Thank you, ma'am."

"No, thank you."

Davies had a good view of the north gate; he could see the crowd outside the gate as it filled the street from one side to the other. In ten minutes, he'd disappear with the wave of visitors as they washed into the fair. The cruller was very good and the coffee wasn't bad. He lit a PLAYERS. *Yes, it will be a very exciting day.*

"I'm too busy to deal with you and the police," Lipschitz said to Alfano.

"Not my problem, let's take a walk."

"Can't, no time."

"Walk, NOW!"

The two men separated themselves from McDunnah and Hayden.

"Here's the straight and skinny, Mr. Lipschitz. There are at least two bombs somewhere in this fair. They will explode today, thousands may die. I am trying to find them and you seem to be in the way. I have two ways to go, either I enlist your help or I get you out of the way. Simple, isn't it? Now, we believe that there is a bomb somewhere near this stage, anybody been poking around this morning?"

"Bomb? Here, stage. Holy shit!"

"Well said, now, think."

"All this construction was finished days ago, sound checks and everything went well. Nothing but cleanup."

A quick series of loud pops exploded over the stadium, everyone jumped. Alfano drew his weapon, seeing the pistol, Lipschitz turned pasty white.

"That was the opening fireworks, in about five minutes we'll be deluged with people trying to get good seats. I suggest we move closer to the stage." Lipschitz began to walk toward the podium, Alfano and his people followed. "Now, where is that oaf?"

"Who?" Alfano asked.

"There was a fellow here to help clean up around the stage; he asked if he could help a few days ago. Then someone who says he's his brother shows up. Told him to go straighten things and clean up around the stage."

"Did he give a name?"

"Said Smith, I think, or something like it. Really couldn't care. Now he's gone, son of a bitch, do you think he had something to do with this?"

"McDunnah, you think this is a coincidence," Alfano said to the sergeant who had moved to his side. "A Smith showing up like this?"

"No fucking way. I'll go and get the bomb expert; he's at the Admin building."

"Is there any way to get under that stage?"

"…From the back, access for the sound people and the wiring, maybe four or five feet of headroom."

"Commissioner, I suggest, at least for the moment, that we close this stadium off before any more people enter, I am going bomb-hunting." Alfano left Hayden and headed to the back of the stage. He heard Hayden giving orders to the security people to close the doors to Soldier Field.

Davies watched the crowd surge into the fair, thousands pushed their way through the gate and onto the grounds, he imagined the same thing was happening at the other gates. Then twenty or so security people quick-marched past him and headed toward the stadium, barricades had been hastily placed across the gates. As the guards passed the gates, three men left the ranks and took positions, they immediately began to turn people away.

"Damn it," Davies said to no one in particular. *They know, damn that Alfano. Maybe he won't find it. Of course he will; damn it all to hell.*

Davies stood, lit another cigarette and began to walk around the lagoon. The crowds built up around him and like riding a small boat on a river, he flowed along with the chattering families and their boisterous, enthusiastic children.

Alfano crawled under the stage; it was dark, hard to see, after a few minutes his eyes grew accustomed to the dim light, nothing was obvious in the tangle of wood and steel substructure. What belongs here and what doesn't? He hadn't a clue. There were small boxes everywhere, wire hung in loops from the underside of the stage. He began to look up into the structure, he could feel the strain on his back as he hunched over, twice he nicked his forehead, he was sure there was a trickle of blood running down his check. After fifteen minutes, he began to doubt his own assumptions, maybe it was elsewhere, buried under the sod, too many places to look. He heard stomping on the stage. Damn it, why the hell would somebody be walking on top of a bomb.

"Tony, where are you?"

"McDunnah, I'm almost directly under you. See anything up there?"

"Nothing, they've closed the gates. We have maybe a half an hour before this all blows up."

"Didn't need that information, McDunnah, really, I didn't."

"Sorry, it came out wrong."

"I know, but it really is dark under here."

"Need a flashlight? That guy, Lipschitz, he brought one out; he says there's a trap door in the middle of the stage, that's why I'm out here. I'll drop it down to you."

Ten feet to Alfano's right, a shaft of light lit the underside of the stage as if a light switch had been thrown.

"Give me one second, I'll catch it," Alfano yelled as he headed toward the light. Half way there, he caught a reflection off metal, "Flashlight."

"Coming down."

Alfano caught it as it fell through the opening and quickly shined the beam on the spot where he'd seen the reflection. A long narrow tool chest sat on a ledge, electrician's tape secured it to a cross-beam. "Found it!"

"Can you get to it?"

"I'm trying now. Do you have a knife?" McDunnah dropped a small penknife through the opening. Alfano cut the tape and gingerly lowered the case to the grass. "Shit."

"What?"

"Metal case with a padlock on it. Need a heavy pair of bolt cutters. Can't do it here. There's a toggle switch on the outside, I assume it's toggled on, logic tells me to click it off."

"Logic tells me to wait for the fucking demolitions expert, Detective. No reason to be a hero, not today. And besides, we still have to find the other one."

"I like your logic. Since it didn't explode when I lowered it, a good bet it won't go off if I move it to the opening. Get ready for it, I'm passing it up."

"Jesus, Mary and Joseph, Tony, I don't want the God damn thing."

"Too bad, reach for it."

Two minutes later, the metal tool chest sat on the floor of the stage, McDunnah and Alfano stood off to one side, about a hundred feet away, waiting for the demolitions expert.

"They've walked the length of the whole stadium and found no one out of place or without the proper credentials. He wasn't inside the stadium."

"No he's out there mixing with the crowd, will be damn hard to find."

They watched the Chicago Police Department's bomb expert snap the lock and open the case, thirty seconds later, he gave everyone the thumbs-up and lifted out the bundle; four of Garon Davis baby-girls.

"One down, Lipschitz, the place is yours. We'll have our men take another look under the stage, but I think there was only one."

"He was carrying a tool chest, so I hope you are right," Lipschitz answered. "I have two hours to get everything ready."

Alfano, Hayden, and McDunnah walked through the tunnel and out into the fair, the sound grew with every step. When they reached the promenade, all McDunnah could say was, "I have never seen this many people in one place in my entire life."

North and south, as far as they could see, there were people, everyone wore expressions of wonder, awe, excitement, and amazement. Heads were upturned, looking toward the buildings and their towers, children pointed at the Sky Ride; the rickshaw boys were already pulling people through the crowds. Even for hardened men like Alfano and McDunnah, the effect was thrilling.

"This is going to be one fucking long day," was all that Alfano could offer. He could barely be heard over the hullabaloo and the rumpus of the fairgoers.

# 34

GARON DAVIES pressed his way through the crowd, he'd snuggled the revolver into the pocket of his baggy pants and left the smaller tool chest under the cruller concession table. It was all falling apart. *I bet by now, that detective found the bomb under the stage; maybe he won't find the truck.* As he walked through the fair, he noticed hundreds of vehicles moving about on the roads behind the buildings, many were parked, many were making deliveries; there were even a few contractors still working on unfinished exhibits. With the influx of visitors, everything was controlled chaos, at best. He had lived in chaos and he would disappear in chaos.

He kept to the side of the lagoon, decorated boats were now filling with patrons eager for their one hour tour on the water, vendors were setting up their concessions, the smell of hot dogs and bratwurst filled the humid air. Even the light mist that was falling couldn't dampen the excitement of the kids as they ran up and down the walkways. He looked at his watch, 10:00, two hours to go.

"Mr. Smythe, is that you?"

The voice struck like a dagger through his heart, he turned to face a young boy looking up at him.

"Mr. Smythe, you look funny. Are you a clown here at the

fair?" Ralph Doolittle asked. "Mother, look, it's Mr. Smythe."

Mrs. Doolittle tilted her head to look at the man her son was pointing to, recognizing him; she pulled Ralph closer to her. "Ralph, that's not Mr. Smythe, Mr. Smythe has gone away, it's not him. I'm certain of it."

"You are Mr. Smythe, aren't you?"

Davies looked into Mrs. Doolittle's eyes and saw a tear, "Young man, I don't know who you are talking about. My name is Davies, Mr. Garon Davies. I work here at the fair."

Mrs. Doolittle immediately understood what was going on. "Ralph, that is not Mr. Smythe. There is some resemblance, that's for sure, but it's not him. I apologize for my son bothering you, sir."

"None needed, he looks to be a fine boy. Now, you two have a wonderful time at the fair, there's so much to see, based on what's here, there's a bonny future ahead for all of us. Good day, madam and good day to you, fella." Davies quickly turned and headed out along the promenade.

"I know he was Mr. Smythe," Ralph said.

"I know what you think, but that was not Mr. Smythe, he said his name was Mr. Davies. Let's get you an ice cream cone, you deserve it." Mrs. Doolittle turned her boy around and climbed the steps to the ice cream parlor.

Davies broke into a cold sweat. He'd been caught. All his sins were laid out instantly before him in the look he'd gotten from Mrs. Doolittle. Every wrong and every justification he'd made in his life, every shortcut, every death, he saw them all in her eyes. His heart pumped hard and loud, he was sure those around him could hear it. Suddenly, every passing glance seemed to silently whisper the word, *murderer*. He retrieved the box of PLAYERS from his pocket; with a shaking hand he lit a cigarette and almost collapsed on a nearby bench.

"You okay, buddy? You look a little strange," a voice said.

Davies looked up, the policeman stood in the brightening

haze of the sun. "Just fine officer, a little too much celebrating last night. I just finished working on our exhibit over there on the other side late last night."

"Why don't you get yourself home and get some sleep? This here fair's going to be here all summer."

"Thank ye, thank ye, that's where I be headed, home." He took another drag on the cigarette and watched the cop walk away.

"There's someone here to see you," McDunnah said to Alfano.

"Who?"

"…Says her name is Doolittle, said she knows you from a couple of days ago."

"Where is she?"

"…Just outside."

Alfano came around the corner of the tent and found Mrs. Doolittle and Ralph standing under the cover of the awning, the mist had started again. "Mrs. Doolittle, I'm surprised to see you here."

"We need to talk; can someone take care of Ralph for a few minutes?"

"Sergeant, can you take this young man over to the security center? I think he'd really like to see what policemen do when they watch over the fair."

McDunnah smiled at Alfano and turned to the young man, "You ever sit in a police car? Well, young man, this is your lucky day."

Alfano turned back to Mrs. Doolittle, "You look shaken up."

"I saw him, Mr. Smythe, I mean Davies. He was just across the lagoon, walking that way, toward the tower. Why is he here, Detective? After all you told me, I'm afraid, very afraid."

"You should be, we are trying to stop him. Why don't you take Ralph home, there's nothing here for him now. Maybe you can bring him back tomorrow. When the sergeant returns, I'll get you some passes for tomorrow, but you should take him home now."

"What about all these other people, they can't all go home."

"We know, that's why we are trying to stop him quickly. So please, Sergeant McDunnah will have someone drive you home."

"No, I'm staying. That man was good to us, kind, I don't believe any of this."

"Please, Mrs. Doolittle, please go."

Ralph and the sergeant returned, "The police car was very exciting, Mother. Where are we going next?"

Mrs. Doolittle looked at Alfano, "We are going to see the dinosaurs; would you like that?"

"...Absolutely."

"What's he wearing?" Alfano asked.

"Why, so you can kill him?"

"... Kill who, Mother?"

"No, because someone is paying him to do it and I want to know who. If we can catch him, maybe it won't go so bad."

"Who, Mother, who?"

"Nothing, Ralph, it's nothing," Alfano said. He looked at Mrs. Doolittle, his eyes pleading with her.

"Workman's clothes, brown and blue, gray fedora, ragged with a hole on the left side, heavy shoes. Please try and save him."

She took the boy by the hand and they walked away into the drizzle.

"Nice kid," McDunnah said, "Nice lady, too."

"Yes, they are, and that fellow, Davies, charmed them. Where the hell is he, Sergeant? Where is he?"

Davies stood with his back to the fair and stared out into the gray waters of Lake Michigan. A lone gull screamed as it drifted away on the wind; he watched as the dark silhouette of a boat and sail broke the crisp line between the sky and the water. He looked at his watch, only one hour to wait. This would be a good place to stand and watch the fireball and the chaos and commotion that would happen shortly after the explosion. He imagined it, the flash first, then maybe two seconds before the sound reached him; the shock wave would crush and pulverize the tower base, it would take a little time, but then the tower would begin to lean, then rotate and fall. Almost as tall as Soldier Field was long, the tower might collapse toward it, taking up the entire length of the stadium. Then the falling cables would put tremendous pressure on the second tower, the one high over this side of the lagoon and it might snap from the tension. The rocket cars would, for a few brief terrorizing seconds, remain airborne before they fell into the lagoon. He was fascinated by all the theater he would cause and all from one well-placed bomb.

He turned back to the lagoon and saw Alfano jogging up the promenade, scanning left and right, frantically looking and searching for him. He moved toward the base of the tower and looked up. *Why not, I've got the time. Across, then down, then head south, away from the tower. Time, I have the time.*

Alfano spotted Davies just as he rounded the concrete base of the tower and head toward the elevators. His jog turned into a sprint as he flashed his badge at the attendant and ran into the first open elevator car, an older couple stood in the corner. They looked at him, then the gun he held at his side. *Not Davies*, he turned to leave, but the door closed before he could jump out. "Shit!"

"Tsk, tsk," the woman whispered.

"Now, Clara, I believe he's a police officer, or at least I

hope he is."

Alfano smiled, "Detective Alfano at your service, doing some training if you understand what I'm saying."

"Young man, I was a cop in Iowa for fifty years, I do understand. Always good to keep up the skills."

Alfano flashed on an idea. "Sir, I need some help, we are conducting an exercise to help understand how to clear the tower in case there's an incident. When we reach the floor where you enter the rocket cars, could you help me direct anyone back to the elevators and have them return to the ground, I know this is an inconvenience but it would be helpful."

"Absolutely, wouldn't mind a bit."

"Bob, are you sure, with your heart and all?"

"Oh Mother, I'm fine, it will be fun."

The doors opened, like a drill sergeant, Alfano watched as Bob announced that they needed to clear the floor and that everyone needed to leave. He pointed to Alfano, Tony held up his badge.

"Please, folks, do as this officer says." Alfano noticed that Bob puffed up a little when he said it.

Alfano watched as the next rocket car slipped into the loading area, back from its trip over the lagoon, maybe twenty people exited. As it passed through the empty loading side, he noticed a shadow quickly enter the car on the far side.

Without hesitation, he ran to the open door of the car and rolled in, pistol out, ready for anything. Garon Davies stood at the back end of the rocket ship, his arm wrapped tightly around a young boy, maybe 10 years old. The car lurched out over the lagoon and began its slow trip east. The rain intensified, the noise echoed through the cabin of the rocket ship.

"Give it up, Davies, there's literally nowhere to go. We're six hundred feet in the air; there are fifty policemen waiting at the other tower. Let the boy go and lay down your gun."

"Can't, you know that. I've got a ticket to California on

Monday and I'll be on that train. Nothing in the world will stop me."

"We have enough time before this car stops, let the boy go. He's scared and you can't take him with you. So let him go."

Davies looked down at the boy and lifted his arm up slowly; the boy slipped under and ran behind Alfano. "Sit there." Alfano pointed at a seat and then looked back at Davies. "Why?"

"Why not, tough to scrape together a stash these days, work for pennies an hour, then stand in line for bread and a cup of soup. I've got a skill, I can make mountains dance and men tremble with fear. Some men paint and create symphonies; I am an artist using Mr. Nobel's invention. His little sticks, my baby-girls, are my instruments. With them, I can create symphonies and arias."

"Songs of death more like it."

"You're a Philistine, you don't understand. This is all for the future, my future. To be paid handsomely for my creations, that's all I ever asked for. I have no moral qualms, no sleepless nights, no worries or fear of a vengeful God." Davies moved to his right, toward the door of the cab.

"Stay right where you are."

"Or what, you'll shoot me in front of the boy, leave him with that memory embedded his head for his whole life. I lived with that my entire life and I would not wish it on anyone. Yes, it's true. When I was a just a lad, I saw my father gunned down by the mill owners and their goons. He died in my arms. It was all my mother could do to raise us and when I could, I left, but I always took care of her until the day she died, she died of a broken heart."

"Then surrender, do it for the boy."

"If I couldn't do it for Ralph, why would I do it for him, he's tough, all kids are tough. Look what they have to put up with, us adults." Davies walked over to the door, it was closed and the lock was secure.

"Please, for the love of God."

As if I haven't heard that one." Davies fired his revolver at the latch; the door flew open as the wind buffeted the car. He quickly swung the gun back at Alfano, "Don't, if you try anything, I don't know where the next bullet will go." He took a step up to the doorway.

"Don't do this, Davies, don't." Alfano walked toward the man; Davies' hat flew back into the cab. "I know someone is paying you, you're their mercenary, their tool. Where's the other bomb? Is that what you really want?"

"Detective Alfano, believe it or not, we are all tools for someone and I always fulfill my contracts." He stood in the door.

"Who is paying you?"

"I really don't know." And he jumped.

Alfano lunged, he caught the pocket of Davies' coat; it ripped as the man fell. Alfano didn't watch, but he heard the screams from the thousands crowded below. He looked at the boy, wide-eyed, speechless. "You okay?"

The boy, in shock, could only nod.

Alfano collapsed into one of the seats; he didn't care about the *No Smoking* sign overhead. He looked at his hand, there was a crushed box of PLAYERS wrapped in the rough cloth of the man's pocket. He managed to find one unbroken cigarette and lit it. Between the box and the fabric, there was also a piece of folded paper. When he opened it, he saw...

*Dear Mr. Smythe,*

*I understand all the difficulties you are going through, I sincerely do. But we must continue to move forward with the plan. Saturday is critical to the contract and its purpose. Through you, Saturday will be my day of vengeance. You will receive your final payment on Sunday morning. I know you will succeed, and those that have sinned will be punished.*

*Sincerely . . . .*

He took another drag and exhaled. His suspicions had been confirmed even as he prayed that he was wrong, the typing proved it. Every letter g had the lower half filled in. The g in vengeance was the darkest as if forced with all the effort of the typist.

# 35

MCDUNNAH was waiting for Alfano at the west tower platform. "We found the rest of the dynamite, your hunch was
right. It was in a painter's truck at the base of this tower."

"An Otto Spellbinder truck?"

"How did you know?"

"...A lucky guess."

"The demolition guy was able to remove the timers and
the caps from the sticks. Said it was one of the best he'd ever
seen. Says the man knew his stuff. Easily a hundred pounds of
the damnable stuff; would have taken down the whole tower
if it had gone off. Was that him that fell?"

"Yes, he jumped."

"Did he tell you who paid him? Who was behind all this?"

"No, not directly, but I know who it is."

"They in City Hall?"

"Yes, very near the top."

Hayden stood to the back of the crowd of police on the
tower's upper landing. The crowd, standing around Alfano,
watched as the parade from downtown worked its way into
Soldier Field; they all wanted a front row seat. Alfano spotted
a boat motoring across the lagoon, loaded with four policemen ready to retrieve the body of Garon Davies. He remembered the look on Davies' face as he jumped, it was surprisingly peaceful.

Alfano walked down the stairs to the terrace just above the lagoon, near the Italian pavilion. A two-thousand-year-old marble column stood just outside the pavilion's doorway; Mussolini had it sent over to celebrate the opening of the fair in honor of all the Italians in Chicago. Alfano's family had come a long way from the craggy hills above the village of Cortona fifty years earlier. America had been good to them.

"Is it over?" she said from behind him.

"Yes, it's over." Tony turned and faced Gini; even though the clouds were spotty, the rain had begun again. Her hair hung damp against her face.

"That's good, now I can have you back, all to myself."

"You know that's not how it's going to work. There are sins to be paid for."

"For some, yes, for others, they always seem to avoid their rightful atonement."

"Like who?"

"It is the simple story of liquor and politics. Think of a young man, arrested four times for drunk driving, still driving a sanitation truck for the City of Chicago. He was also Edward Kelly's neighbor's son. Edward Kelly was the head of the Sanitation Department of Chicago, both were from Bridgeport, after each arrest, Mr. Kelly made sure the boy got his job back driving trucks for the city. One morning, after he had been drinking at a bar called Jimmy's, he climbed into his garbage truck and began his rounds. Occasionally, he took a sip from a bottle in his pocket; the boy's name *was* Timothy O'Toole. As he passed a small park, a child was playing with his new puppy, my child, my Thaddeus, and the puppy ran out into the road and the boy chased the puppy and the boy was killed." At this point, Gini was in tears, reliving that day; Alfano went to put his arm around her. "Don't! The whole police force could have done something and they did nothing. So don't you touch me, Anthony Alfano, don't you dare." She took a deep breath. "After the child was buried, an alderman came by to console the mother, he understood what had happened and thought this would be a great way to get to the mayor, through the head of the sanitation department. But all the alderman really wanted was to romance the poor woman and take advantage of her; in a drunken fit, he raped her, then he went home to his family. Then she went to the *Tribune* to tell them the story, they were interested for a while, sad about the whole affair, then the story died, they could have made something of it, but they didn't. They had an opportunity to put their power up against City Hall and they walked away, especially the arrogant publisher, McCormick. At least Alderman Polk, in a moment of remorse, I guess, had pity on the woman and helped her get a job in city hall. In time, she became Cermak's secretary; he was an okay guy as a boss but a very, very bad boy as mayor. One day, he said, 'Can you put this in the safe?' She said, 'What safe?' he pointed the wall, 'behind the new president.' He also gave her the combination. I guess he figured if anything was missing he'd know who to look for." She reached into her bag, extracted a gold case and lit a cigarette. "Like it? A gift from Anton Cermak, well at least he paid for it. On the day everyone heard he was killed, she went to the safe and took four bundles of bills that he had placed there, $200,000, all nice and old and wrapped in neat little wrappers. She never knew who it belonged to. It became her personal vengeance fund. And then a month later, she became Edward Kelly's personal secretary."

"You need some help, Gini. Please let me help."

"I can assure you that I am the last person anyone can help. So I worked very hard on a plan and I acquired the services of a discrete man who would be my sword of vengeance, like those queens of old who had a man of honor and steel at the ready to protect them and vanquish evil. Mr. Smythe was that man, that knight, for me."

"He told me he didn't know who hired him."

"That is correct, he never did know. In fact, I never met

the man; we did everything through the post office, quite effective. So it began, I provided him with my list of locations and the order in which the tasks would need to be accomplished. He was very good, don't you think? He stayed ahead of you for almost a month and until a few days ago you never had a clue to his identity. It was his association and friendship with that young boy that was his downfall. Sadly, my son died while her son lives. So my path to achieving total vengeance was set and now we end up here, but the complete job is unfinished."

"What can I do to help you, anything?"

"Well, in about five minutes, the mayor will be speaking, welcoming the world to Chicago, you could just walk up to him and shoot him for me. That would make me feel a little better."

Alfano didn't understand what was happening, this woman was not the woman he had loved or thought he knew. She was like a chameleon, first one person then another. But he now understood her heart had never healed. All the efforts expended to find happiness or acceptance since Tad's death had been for nothing. She would die a broken woman.

"You know I have to arrest you, I have no choice."

"I know. We each have important roles in this play, you have your path laid out for you and I have mine." Gini slipped her hand into her purse and removed a small .38 revolver. The chrome flashed in a brief moment of sunshine.

Alfano raised both his hands. "Don't do this, Gini, you can't escape. Look around you, there's hundreds of police standing around, watching us, there is no way out for you."

Gini looked at the gun and then at Alfano, "You think this is meant for you or to help me escape? No, Tony, my dearest love, this is for my son—and me."

She turned the pistol toward her chest, pulled the trigger and put a bullet through her once broken heart.

# 36

THE NEXT MORNING, Sunday, Mrs. Doolittle, still exhausted from all the questions that were asked by the police concerning Garon Davies and the plot to blow up the Century of Progress Fair, started breakfast. To Alfano's credit, he came to her defense and she was allowed to go home with her son. They realized that she knew nothing about any of Davies' actions or his connections to anyone else. Ralph was thrilled with his day spent at the fair and by the time the fireworks exploded over the Lake Michigan, he could barely keep his eyes open. After the questioning, Anthony Alfano drove the Doolittles home.

Sunday was a quiet day and she slept until 7:00, a luxury for her. She was drinking her coffee when the doorbell rang. A man stood in the door; it was her regular postman.

"What are you doing here delivering on a Sunday?"

"I traded with a fellow so I could go to the fair yesterday, I'm doing Special Deliveries today. Did you hear about the man who fell from the Sky Ride, it happened just before we arrived, everyone was talking about it. What a way to start the fair."

"Yes, we were on the other side. Thank the Lord that Ralph didn't see what happened." She looked at the letter in the postman's hand. "Special Delivery for me, why, I never."

"Well, that's what it says. And I know that's your name. So Mrs. Doolittle, just sign here and I can go to my next stop."

She signed his pad and took the letter into the kitchen; it was lumpy.

She took a knife and cut open the envelope, three keys and a letter fell out of it. She unfolded the letter; she noticed that it was dated yesterday.

*May 27, 1933*

*Dear Loraine,*

*There is an excellent chance that I may be dead by now. That is the price I might pay in the line of work that I have pursued for the last forty or so years. And it's a price that I accept. You have heard, by now, horrific stories about me and what I have done. I am sorry that I have put you and Ralph through all that. You are one of the most honorable and kindest people I have ever known and you deserve more than what the fates have handed you.*

*You have been wronged. The city was very hard on you and Ralph and there should be some form of restitution.*

*Here is what I would like you to do. In an alley four blocks away, located between Horton and Lime Streets, there is a garage that I rented a few months back, it is behind the third house and sits up against the railroad tracks that run through that part of the neighborhood. The enclosed large key is for the side door; inside you'll find a lot of my things that I have used for my last month's activities. There are no explosives left in the building. On the workbench, you'll find a carpenter's ruler, measure six feet from the back of the garage and twelve feet from the face of the work bench. Dig down about six inches and you will find a heavy steel door and another padlock. Use the smaller key to unlock it. Open the lid, you will find some suitcases and other paraphernalia, you will have no need of the guns or the rifle that are there, leave them. Take the leather suitcase out and take it with you. Close the steel door, relock the cover and then relock the garage. When you are able, please go the Central Post office and go to*

*Box 2513, use the 2ⁿᵈ smaller key and see if another small bundle has been placed there. You will also find an envelope in that post box with your name on it. Inside are two tickets to California and the address of a very nice house overlooking the ocean near a town called Santa Monica and a key. Everything in the leather suitcase, the postal package and the envelope is for you and Ralph. Do not fret about the money, no one will miss it. I don't know its source, but I am fairly certain it does not have a reputable past. Have a wonderful life and think of me now and then. We are never gone if someone remembers us once in a while.*

*Most sincerely,*
*Garon L. Davies*

The End

A Note from the Author:

Gregory C. Randall is the author of the Tony Alfano detective series. Mr. Randall has authored numerous works of fiction including the Sharon O'Mara Chronicles and the award winning young adult book, Elk River.

Gregory C. Randall was born in Traverse City, Michigan and grew up in Chicago. Greg has never forgotten his roots. Now a Californian by choice, Mr. Randall makes his home in Walnut Creek, California with his wife.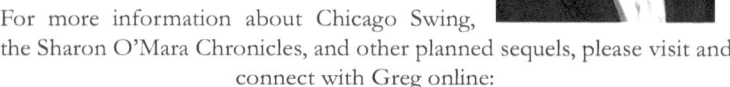

Mr. Randall is the author of fiction and non-fiction works available through the usual outlets and the Windsor Hill Publishing website.

For more information about Chicago Swing, the Sharon O'Mara Chronicles, and other planned sequels, please visit and connect with Greg online:
http://www.gregorycrandall.com
http://www.gregorycrandall.info
and see his blog:
http://www.writing4death.blogspot.com

Other books by Mr. Randall available both in print and as ebooks:

Fiction
Elk River

The Sharon O'Mara Chronicles
Land Swap For Death
Containers For Death
Toulouse For Death
12th Man For Death
Diamonds For Death

Non-fiction
America's Original GI Town, Park Forest, Illinois

These books can be purchased through Amazon, CreateSpace, and IngramSpark.

Enjoy!

www.ingramcontent.com/pod-product-compliance
Lightning Source LLC
Chambersburg PA
CBHW022042240626
47154CB00007B/2524